Terror in Philadelphia

The cacophonous clatter of hooves slowly began to fade. After what seemed like an eternity, it disappeared altogether.

Jonathan helped Mindy dismount, and Mindy pulled the chronolyzer, a futuristic PDA, from out of the hem of her skirt, powering on the device.

"Chronolyzer, what the hell was that . . . thing chasing us?" Mindy asked worriedly.

I'M NOT TALKING TO YOU, it displayed.

"What do you mean? You can't refuse to give information—you're a computer.

A STOLEN COMPUTER. THOUGH YOU'RE RIGHT—I DO HAVE TO ANSWER. BUT MAY I FIRST SUGGEST THAT YOU TURN YOURSELVES INTO DEWITT AT ONCE? YOUR CHANCES OF EVADING AN INTELLIGENCE OFFICER AND A CYBER-BLOODHOUND ARE MICROSCOPICALLY SMALL.

"Just answer my question," Mindy snapped. "We've heard about enough of your opinions."

NO NEED TO BE TESTY. NO DOUBT I'LL SOON BE IN THE POSSESSION OF SOMEONE MORE PRUDENT THAN EITHER OF YOU. DEWITT'S HORSE IS A CYBER-BLOODHOUND. IT HAS A METALLIC ENDOSKELETON THAT ALLOWS IT TO TRANSFORM INTO ANY PERIOD-APPROPRIATE ANIMAL.

"So it's a robot?"

CYBORG, ACTUALLY. IT'S PART ANIMAL, PART ROBOT.

"Maybe we should get out of the street," Jonathan said.

SOUND LOGIC, PREACHER MAN, THE CHRONOLYZER TYPED. THE CYBER-BLOODH-PUND WAS MADE TO HUNT ALIEN BEASTIES FAR MORE CRAFT AND RESOURCEFUL THAN THE TWO OF YOU. INSIDE IS GOOD, BECAUSE BY MY CALCULATIONS, IF YOU STAY OUTSIDE THERE IS A 98.3 PERCENT LIKELIHOOD THAT THE CYBER-BLOODHOUND WILL FIND YOU AND CRUSH EVERY BONE IN YOUR BODY WITHIN TEN MINUTES.

All titles in the **Smart Novels** series:

SAT Vocabulary

Busted

Head Over Heels

Sun-Kissed

Vampire Dreams

Rave New World

S.C.A.M.

U.S. History

Volume I: A Time for Witches

Volume II: Shades of Blue and Gray

Volume III: Reckless Revolution

Volume IV: Gilded Delirium

smart novels
U.S. HISTORY

Reckless Revolution

Volume III

by Lynne Hansen

SPARKNOTES is a registered trademark of SparkNotes LLC.

Spark Publishing
A Division of Barnes & Noble
120 Fifth Avenue
New York, NY 10011
www.sparknotes.com

ISBN-13: 978-1-4114-9672-9
ISBN-10: 1-4114-9672-8

Library of Congress Cataloging-in-Publication Data

Hansen, Lynne, 1968–
  Reckless revolution / by Lynne Hansen.
      p. cm.—(Smart Novels)
   Summary: Twentieth-century teenager Mindy Gold, seventeenth-century minister Jonathan Hartthorne, and twenty-second-century "time cop" Jasper Gordon time-travel to 1775 Philadelphia, where they face rabble-rousing Whigs, smallpox outbreaks, and carnivorous pigs as they search for an alien and its captive.
   ISBN-13: 978-1-4114-9672-9
   ISBN-10: 1-4114-9672-8
   [1. Time travel—Fiction. 2. Boardinghouses—Fiction. 3. Quakers—Fiction. 4. Smallpox—Fiction. 5. Extraterrestrial beings—Fiction. 6. Philadelphia (Pa.)—History—Colonial period, ca. 1600-1775--Fiction. 7. United States—History—Revolution, 1775-1783—Causes—Fiction. 8. Science fiction.] I. Title.
   PZ7.H198252Con 2007
   [Fic]—dc22

                                                                                      2007019275

Please submit changes or report errors to www.sparknotes.com/errors.

Printed and bound in the United States.

10 9 8 7 6 5 4 3 2 1

CONTENTS

FROM THE CHRONOLYZER'S HARD DRIVE:

The Story So Far . . .

In *A Time for Witches,* Mindy Gold is sent back in time by a device called a *chronobomb* detonated by a mysterious being named Andros. Mindy's sister Serena and several of her classmates are also within range of the blast, and each of them is sent back to a different time and place in American history. Finding herself in 1692 Salem at the height of the Salem Witch Trial hysteria, Mindy is approached by Jasper Gordon, a time-cop from the future. Jasper explains that Andros is the agent of the Galagians, an alien race of time travelers that can possess the bodies of human beings. Andros's chronobomb not only sent Mindy and her friends back in time, it also created pathways for the Galagians to enter the human time stream. Jasper enlists Mindy's help in finding her friends and sending them back to their own time while expelling the Galagians from the humans they have taken possession of.

Mindy and Jasper are quickly arrested by the Salem authorities on suspicion of witchcraft, and the only person willing to aid them is Jonathan Hartthorne, a nineteen-year-old Puritan minister and naturalist. When Mindy and Jasper finally use Jasper's chronolyzer to escape to the future, they unwittingly take the young minister with them.

In *Shades of Blue and Gray,* Mindy and Jasper travel to the Civil War Battle of Bull Run in pursuit of Andros, who has stolen Jonathan Hartthorne's body and fled with it to 1865 Virginia. There they discover Mindy's friend Chad, who was sent into the past by the chronobomb and trapped inside the body of a Union soldier. Mindy and Jasper track Andros to a medical camp where he is impersonating a doctor, in the process freeing Chad and Jonathan. They return Chad to his own time but receive orders from Jasper's mysterious superiors not to return Minister Hartthorne to his.

Now, Mindy, Jasper, and Jonathan go to Revolutionary Philadelphia to rescue Mindy's sister Serena—unless Andros gets to her first.

CHARACTERS

Mindy Gold. A seventeen-year-old girl from modern-day Salem, Massachusetts.

Serena Gold. Mindy's younger sister, who is sent back in time at the same time as Mindy, but to 1775 Philadelphia.

Jasper Gordon. A young time-policeman from the twenty-sixth century. The chronopolice possess powerful technology and serve a totalitarian state in the future. There seems to be more to Jasper than meets the eye, though, as he often operates outside of Future State protocols.

Jonathan Hartthorne. A nineteen-year-old minister from colonial Salem, accidentally brought with Jasper and Mindy into the future.

The chronolyzer. A sentient, handheld communication and information device. The chronolyzer can transport you in time, provide you with appropriate period costumes, and tell you whatever you need to know about the period you're in—but with an obnoxious attitude.

Andros. A mysterious being working for the Galagians. Whether Andros is a Galagian or something else is unclear. Andros can time-travel and take possession of people's bodies.

The Galagians. Aliens who exist outside of time, and who seek human bodies to inhabit. They can only possess humans who have *tempose* in their blood, a substance that most humans produce in the future, but few or none do in the past. Unfortunately, Andros can make humans in the past habitable to the aliens.

Chapter One

Mindy Gold hated the way time travel poked at her from the inside out. Not that she'd done a ton of history-hopping, but now visiting her third different era, the seventeen-year-old knew each trip was (a) always different and (b) always annoying. On this occasion, time travel felt like someone had tossed two handfuls of corn into a fireplace. The only problem was that the fireplace was her stomach, and each exploding kernel seemed to ricochet against her brain. As she plummeted through time, the popcorn charred as if it had been left in a microwave too long, and when she arrived in the past, the popcorn transformed into real smoke.

Mindy coughed and gagged. It appeared she'd been transported into a burning building. Through the smoke, she quickly scanned the cramped, austere bedroom. The unembellished wardrobe closet, knobby bed, and roughhewn wooden desk and chair looked vaguely colonial, but there wasn't anything in this room that would allow Mindy to firmly identify her location. The furniture seemed like it might be at home in a wealthy family's 1630s cottage or a poor person's 1830s crash pad.

Coughing, the rugged minister, Jonathan Hartthorne, came to her side, his wavy, shoulder-length brown hair wafting behind him as if he'd been strutting into a fashion photographer's wind machine. The Puritan minister's emerald green eyes were tinged with worry. "Mindy, did you arrive unscathed?"

"I think so," said Mindy. "Where's Jasper?"

Jasper Gordon, the sprightly, irreverent, and occasionally foul-mouthed time-cop who led their forays into the past, was not always the most reliable companion. A mysterious figure who seemed constantly at odds with his own agency, Jasper had a tendency to flit off to God-knows-where when Mindy and Jonathan needed him the most.

An indistinct crash filtered through an open window behind them.

"He was with us when the chronolyzer transported us from 2512," Jonathan said. "He must be here somewhere."

It was odd hearing a Puritan minister from 1692 talk so casually about time travel, but nothing about Jonathan Hartthorne was typical. The rugged clergyman looked like he'd waltzed off the cover of a trashy romance novel. He had a square jaw, complete with the requisite chin dimple, and muscles that would put any of the jocks on the Salem High School football team to shame. And he was reliable—unlike their missing-in-action time-cop leader.

"Jasper!" Mindy called.

A muffled response came from the unadorned wardrobe closet along the wall. "Jasper?"

No answer.

Mindy flung open the door. A slender little man with curly brown hair, handsome in a delicate and almost girlish way, was hunched inside, studying a handheld device. He peered at his glowing chronolyzer screen, his knees tucked beneath his chin. The Time Stream Investigator looked up at Mindy with a twinkle in his eye and said in his rich, musical brogue, "Chronolyzer, period clothes for the lot us, if you please."

Jasper Gordon, the feisty Time Stream Investigator from 2512 who'd yanked Mindy from her comfortable-yet-boring life in twenty-first-century Salem, would have been cute—if he weren't quite so irresponsible.

Voices came in through the window—the muffled, commanding shout of a man, followed by the darkly ardent support of a crowd.

As Jasper disentangled himself from the wardrobe closet, the chronolyzer (the Swiss Army knife of future electronic organizers) dissolved Mindy's jeans and T-shirt, replacing them with a plain, long, rust-colored over-dress that parted in the middle to reveal a white linen petticoat. The bodice of the gown was snugger than her twenty-first-century prom dress had been, but at least the stays were more forgiving than the corset she'd worn during her Civil War travels.

"The building is on fire, and you're worried about dialing our clothing receivers to period clothes?" Mindy said.

New attire melted onto Jonathan and Jasper's bodies as well—long-sleeved white linen shirts, snug vests that came to their upper thighs, and closely cut knee-length coats. Their tight linen breeches were met at their knees by stockings. The only difference between the two young men was that Jasper's coat was chestnut brown while Jonathan's was a dark blue that set off his ever-expressive emerald eyes.

"Speaking as someone whose last time trip was done without a clothing receiver," Jonathan said, "I believe we should give thanks."

"It's not like clothes were in short supply during the Civil War," Mindy said. During their last trip, Minister Hartthorne's naked body had been hijacked by the mysterious Andros and taken back to the Battle of Bull Run.

"Perhaps *you* could convince a Confederate soldier to part with his uniform, but I don't share that skill." He grinned.

Mindy felt the heat rise to her cheeks. "Okay, okay, so I'm thankful, but right now breathing smoke-free air is a bit more pressing."

"Sure and there's no need to be hasty," Jasper said, smiling. "We'll just open the other window and get a wee bit of fresh air and take the lay of the land." More irate voices tumbled into the room. "Right, and that would explain the smoke."

Mindy and Jonathan peered out the window over Jasper's shoulder. A crowd surrounded a smoldering bonfire in the middle of the cobblestone street. An army of citizens carried items from the house and added them to the fire.

An older man in his mid-fifties struggled against two strong-armed young men in their twenties. He spat in the direction of a man surveying the mayhem from the stoop of the house.

"Let me go! You can't do this to me, Conrad Flaugh. I worked hard for these things."

"What are they doing?" Mindy asked.

Jonathan leaned down and pointed at the man on the stoop. "That man Conrad seems to be the leader. Whatever is going on, my guess is he's the instigator."

Unlike the majority of the men in the crowd, Conrad wore a powdered wig. Silver buttons ran down the front of his finely tailored olive suit. He held himself stiffly upright with a cool detachment. "If you wanted to keep your goods, Thomas, you should have purchased colonial commodities, not British ones."

The crowd rumbled in approval.

"Are we not all British subjects?" Thomas asked. "What difference does it make if I buy goods manufactured here or in Britain? And what business is it of yours, Conrad?"

A chorus of "Tory!" rolled through the mob.

"Take it all," Conrad growled. "We'll burn every last piece of contraband." He strutted into the house. Half a dozen men from the crowd surged in after him.

"We need to get out of here before this Conrad jerk decides to burn the whole place down," Mindy said.

"Just grab some of this shite that's laying about," Jasper said. "We'll toss it on the fire like everyone else as we leave. Sure and who'll notice the difference?"

Minister Hartthorne frowned. "I will not intentionally destroy a man's property."

"I'm with Jonathan," Mindy said. "Besides, we don't know exactly what they're burning."

"What does it matter?" Jasper said. "We're only here to find and capture that fecker Andros and his slimy Galagian crony—"

"And one of my friends, whom Andros just happened to send back as well," Mindy interjected.

Jasper tugged at his collar uncomfortably. "Em. Right. But in order to do that, standard Time Stream Investigator protocol dictates that we get to a safe place and consult with the chronolyzer to get our bearings. Sure and the most efficient way to do that is to blend in with the local inhabitants."

Mindy rolled her eyes. The Time Stream Investigator could care less about following bureaucratic TSI procedures, except when they allowed him to do what he wanted, and right now, for whatever reason, he obviously wanted to go mingle with the indigenous population.

Jonathan cleared his throat. "Or we could leave out the back."

"Sounds like a plan to me," said Mindy. "Let's go."

"What? That's not a bloody plan!" Jasper said.

"It's two against one. You're outvoted," Mindy said, turning her back on the time-cop. To be honest, running out the back door probably wasn't much of a plan, but she'd consider any option that kept them away from the angry mob out front.

Mindy tried to keep her eyes off the hunky minister's backside as he led the way down two flights of narrow stairs, but she had to watch her feet to prevent tripping over her long linen petticoats, and Jonathan's well-sculpted calves were in her direct line of sight. Keeping her gaze averted was more of a challenge than breathing in her tight dress.

They reached the ground floor without Mindy taking a nosedive or drooling on the minister, and just as Jonathan had predicted, nothing stood between them and the back door.

"Looks like everyone's out front," Mindy said, trying to keep her voice from sounding smug.

"Bloody wonderful," Jasper said.

But as Jonathan reached for the doorknob, a strident voice called from behind them, freezing them in their tracks.

"Oy, you three! Stop!"

From the chronolyzer's hard drive . . .

Philadelphia Stories:

6 Historical Tidbits About the City of Brotherly Love

Sure, we all know that Philly is the birthplace of our great nation. It's also the birthplace of a boxing movie franchise that won't go away and a delicious sandwich. But there's more to Philadelphia's history than *Rocky* and cheese-steaks.

Tidbit #1: Philadelphia's first European settlers were Swedes

We'll start off short and Swede. The first European settlers in the area that would become Philadelphia were not the English—who founded the city in 1682—but the Swedish, who, along with immigrants from Germany, the Netherlands, and Finland, began farming the area in 1538. The Swedish residents of the colony of New Sweden enjoyed some degree of autonomy until England's King Charles II granted the land to William Penn for his colony of Pennsylvania in the 1680s. Lucky for them, Penn welcomed all types of settlers in his new colony, and the Swedes, Germans, Finns, and Dutch eventually melded into the larger English population. Now that's a Swede deal!

Tidbit #2: Philadelphia got off to a "shaky" start

The original English settlers of Philadelphia were best known for three things: peace, tolerance, and violent shaking. Originally, the majority of the early English settlers were members of the Religious Society of Friends, also known as the Quakers. *Quaker* was a derisive term meant to mock the way the group's members, during their religious meetings, would shake (or quake) with religious fervor. Rather than taking offense, the peace-loving Christian sect accepted *Quaker* as an alternate name and advised others to "tremble at the word of God." Founder William Penn envisioned both Philadelphia and the state of Pennsylvania as places where his fellow Quakers could do a whole lot of shakin' without interference.

Tidbit #3: Pennsylvania was *not* named for founder William Penn

With a name like *Penn*sylvania, it's only natural to assume that the state is named for its founder, William Penn, right? Actually, the province was named originally for William Penn's father. In 1681, the younger Penn—seeking a secure homeland for his fellow Quakers—applied for a land grant from England's King Charles II. The king complied, largely to settle a huge monetary debt he owed to Penn's father, the famous admiral Sir William Penn. The younger Penn wanted to call his American province *Sylvania*, which is Latin for "wooded place." The king, however, insisted that it be named in honor of the elder Penn. A number of possible name combinations were suggested, including *Pennvania, Sylpenn,* and *Pennsyl,* before the two settled on *Pennsylvania*.

Tidbit #4: Philadelphia's William Penn is *not* the guy on the oats box

A lot of Philly residents are apt to brag that their city founder is the familiar, smiling old man of Quaker Oats box fame. We're sorry to burst their bubbles, but it's just not true. Actually, the friendly face that has greeted generations of breakfast eaters belongs to no one special. It's just the likeness of an actor from Chicago hired by the Quaker Oats Company when it redid its logo in the 1950s. So what did Penn really look like? Well, according to his best-known portrait, he looked a lot like the Quaker Oats guy!

Tidbit #5: The U.S. Marines were born in a Philadelphia tavern

Drinking establishments have given rise to many a great American institution, including beer pong, beer checkers, and . . . the U.S. Marines? It's true. America's bravest can trace their origin back to a waterfront bar in Philadelphia called Tun Tavern. Built in 1685, it was a favorite meeting place for Ben Franklin, George Washington, Thomas Jefferson, and other delegates to the Continental Congress, who used it as an ad hoc committee room. In 1775, the Congress commissioned Samuel Nicholas as Captain of Marines and charged him with raising the first two battalions. Nicholas established his headquarters at the recruiting office in Tun Tavern. If you'd like to pay respect to the historic site today, be prepared to dodge traffic: The bar was torn down to make way for Interstate 95.

Tidbit #6: Philadelphia was the site of one of General Washington's biggest military blunders

Everybody makes mistakes—even our founding fathers. During the Revolutionary War, Washington made a serious tactical boo-boo that caused Americans to lose the city of Philadelphia to the British. It went something like this: Washington and his troops took up a defensive position on the eastern shore of the Brandywine River, a tributary of the Christina River southwest of Philadelphia, while sending detachments and sentries to guard other crossings to the south and to the north. British general Sir William Howe sent a detachment as if to engage Washington in battle, while looping his main force north, where they crossed the river with no trouble. Then he marched south and surprised the Americans with a full-on attack. Lucky for us, Washington was able to regain control of the city the next year. If he hadn't, we'd be enjoying Philly bangers and mash instead of Philly cheesesteaks.

Chapter Two

Mindy turned to find Conrad frowning at them.

"What did you find upstairs?" Conrad demanded. He had the voice of a man in charge. Beneath a powdered wig, Conrad arched an eyebrow at her. "Well?"

They hadn't found anything, but maybe if she lied about it, the man would leave them be, but maybe he wouldn't and then—

Jasper straightened his shoulders and shrugged. "Not a thing."

Conrad regarded the three of them, narrowing his gaze. Mindy held her breath.

"Blasted Tory. I know Thomas is hiding more imported British goods than what we've got on the fire. Try the woodshed out back. If nothing else, we'll have some more fuel."

"Will do," Jasper said, leading Mindy and Minister Hartthorne out the back door.

"Sheesh, that was close!" Mindy said as they stepped out into the warm midday sun. She breathed deeply. The air smelled even stronger of smoke.

"I would have rather spent a little time chatting with him, but Conrad didn't really seem like a sociable kind of fellow." Jasper patted his jacket searching for something.

"So what's the date?" Mindy asked.

"Hold your horses, Gold, I'll have it in a minute," Jasper said.

Jasper Gordon's normal job—at least, as he'd explained it to Mindy—was essentially border patrol for the time stream, and because the TSI unit was good at keeping aliens from invading human history and wreaking havoc on the time stream, the job had been pretty boring—until recently.

Just over a week ago, a particularly nasty agent of the Galagian aliens named Andros had managed to cross the time stream. Bored with body-hopping alone through history, he'd detonated a chrono-bomb in the middle of a cluster of present-day Salem, Massachusetts, teenagers, sending Mindy's sister and some of her classmates back into America's past, where their spirits served as a kind of landing platform for Galagians hoping to invade that past too.

Andros's chronobomb had bound an undetermined number of twenty-first-century teens to an equal number of Andros's alien friends and blasted them into human host bodies throughout history. Now Mindy and Jonathan were helping the TSI Unit locate the missing teens and return them to their own times. If Andros found them first, he would free his alien friends and vanquish Mindy's friends to the Void. Jasper, Mindy, and Jonathan had to find the teens before Andros did.

"So, chronolyzer," Jasper said as he pulled the seemingly omni-scient device from his pocket, "when are we, exactly?"

MAY 9, 1775, the chronolyzer typed.

Jonathan rubbed his palms on his dark blue breeches. "Eighty-three years in the future for me."

"And over two-hundred-and-thirty years in the past for me," Mindy said.

AND PRECISELY 737 YEARS IN THE PAST FOR ME, THE CHRONOLYZER DISPLAYED. NOT THAT I GET THE SAME KICK OUT OF ADDITION AND SUBTRACTION THAT YOU ALL

SEEM TO. PERHAPS I SHOULD REPLACE MYSELF WITH A CALCULATOR—OR MAYBE AN ABACUS—BECAUSE THAT'S HOW MUCH OF MY CAPACITY YOU'RE CURRENTLY UTILIZING.

"Any time you're bloody ready," muttered Jasper irritably. He and his chronolyzer never seemed to get along.

Mindy backed away, palms up. "Jonathan, you're a witness. I was trying to play nice, and the chronolyzer started in on *me*. Just because I'm from the twenty-first century doesn't mean I'm some slack-jawed yokel."

Jasper sighed. "Never mind, Mindy. The machine just thinks it's joking with you. In order to attain true sentience, they have to program the bastard things with a sense of humor, or they won't work."

"It's not a joke if it's not funny," Mindy said. "The lives of my friends are at stake here."

"Just try to think of it as an irritating friend that you put up with because he's your boyfriend's younger brother."

YOU'D BETTER BE NICE TO ME OR I WON'T LET YOU USE MY NEW FEATURE.

"So?"

SO I CAN NOW TRIANGULATE THE PRECISE LOCATION OF THE ALIEN AND THE TEENAGER WHOSE SPIRIT IT HIJACKED—

"Amazing!" Mindy said.

—WITHIN A RANGE OF ONE HUNDRED FEET, WITH AN ACCURACY RATE OF 90 PERCENT.

Mindy's shoulders fell, while Jasper cocked his head thoughtfully, considering the possibilities. "Sure and it's not perfect, but all we have to do is walk the perimeter to narrow the location and reduce the number of potential host bodies."

"It's a freakin' GPS, Jasper! It took you people five hundred years to *reinvent* a global positioning system?"

Jonathan knitted his eyebrows. "And what in blazes is a global—"

"You give it coordinates, and it'll direct you to wherever you want to go."

"Sure except the chronolyzer doesn't need coordinates," Jasper said. "Since the missing teen and alien are bound to the same body, it will be able to locate the hijacked teen based on the Galagian specifications I've provided."

"Did you see that mob out front? The range is too wide to do any good. We'll be lucky to narrow it down to a block, much less a particular person."

Jonathan put his hand on Mindy's shoulder and lowered his voice. "We must try, Mindy, for your friends' sakes."

The minister's hand felt warm and comforting. As frustrating as the situation was, as long as she had Jonathan, Mindy knew she'd make it through. "Okay," Mindy said. "What do we do?"

Follow the blinking green dot on the screen, the chronolyzer typed.

The chronolyzer led them around the corner of the brick house and into the crowd. The bonfire flared with scorched contraband. The mob whooped and cheered the destruction as someone clanked pots and pans together in an almost festive fashion. Mindy pitied Thomas as he helplessly watched his meager household possessions added onto the bonfire. Still, she couldn't help feeling relieved that just this once they weren't the center of the negative attention.

A portly woman climbed the stoop in front of the brick home next door. She wore a simple, dark-colored Quaker dress covered by a white apron. A white cap covered her head, and a handkerchief had been wrapped around her neck and tucked into the collar of her dress. She addressed the inflamed crowd with controlled contempt. "Have none of you a single thought in your knowledge box?"

"He's a Tory, Widow Madison!" someone shouted.

"We found enumerated goods!" said another.

The mob clamored in support to clattering pots and pans.

"Enumerated goods?" Widow Madison said, snorting. "You mean the bit of tea you've thrown on the fire? Some brightly colored cloth? A few ribbons and lacy things made in Britain? Do you all have nothing better to do with your time?"

Mindy cringed at Widow Madison's audacity, but she admired it too. It took an awful lot to face down an angry mob like that. This woman wasn't even breaking a sweat—it was like she ate guys like Conrad for breakfast, while reading the paper.

Thomas's watery blue eyes blazed. "Finally, someone with enough gumption to stand up for the Crown."

"I'm standing up for my friend and neighbor," Widow Madison said, "not the Crown."

Conrad stepped forward, ever the patriot firebrand. "Good thing you are not, Widow Madison. You know British goods are strictly forbidden. The non-consumption ordinance has been in effect since March first of this year, throughout America. It is the law."

Widow Madison eyed him disdainfully. "Conrad Flaugh . . . I should have known you for the bellwether of this jaunt. You are burning Thomas's meager possessions because he has a few British baubles among them?"

Conrad narrowed his gaze. "He does not simply *have* enumerated goods. He is *selling* them."

A young man in his mid-twenties appeared at Widow Madison's side. "To whom?" he demanded.

Widow Madison tried to gesture him away. "Samuel, no."

Samuel's muscular physique strained at the covered buttons of his well-worn brown linsey suit. His wavy brown hair was tied at the nape of his neck, and, like Widow Madison, he had a genuine yet intense demeanor. He refused to be silenced and insisted on standing up for Widow Madison and Thomas. "Even if Thomas *did* have British goods, no one in this neighborhood has enough specie to buy his imports."

Thomas shifted uneasily from foot to foot, no longer defiantly meeting the accusing gazes of the crowd.

"We caught him in the act," Conrad said. "He was about to deliver a crate of illegal tea when we stopped him."

"I see no crate of tea on that fire. Where is it now?" Widow Madison said. "Leave my neighbor be. Disperse and attend to your own affairs."

Mindy was amazed at Widow Madison's crusty assertiveness.

"The cause of liberty *is* our affair," Conrad said, adding ominously, "and it should be yours too."

Samuel puffed up and leaned forward. "Widow Madison is a Quaker. She may not believe in violence, but she is no Tory, and you know it."

Widow Madison frowned. "You do not need to defend my beliefs, Samuel. It is my Inner Light that I listen to, not some mob."

Conrad snorted. "You'd better be listening to the Continental Association, or you'll find yourself in a Continental Coat." Tin pots and pans rattled encouragement as the crowd rallied.

Mindy didn't know what a Continental Coat was, but she didn't want to find out. As she watched the tense confrontation, sparks and glowing debris from the small conflagration wafted upward, some of it finding purchase on the shingles above the stoop. Too focused on the bonfire and the argument between Conrad and Widow Madison, the crowd didn't seem to notice.

Mindy whispered to Jasper, "Has the chronolyzer narrowed it down at all? This is starting to turn ugly."

Jonathan frowned. "It's been ugly. People should not treat each other this way."

Jasper spoke up. "Sure and the missing teen's host body is either one of these irate Philadelphians or someone inside the boarding-house. Since the chronolyzer transported us into a house instead of onto the street, I'm guessing the missing teen is inside the boardinghouse."

Tilting his head to the side, Jonathan said, "Would that be the house that's ablaze?"

Founding Father Follies:

7 Little-Known Facts About America's Founding Fathers

We tend to think of the founding fathers as perfect, almost godlike guys. But even the greatest patriots have their quirks.

Little-known fact #1: James Madison was vertically challenged

At only five-foot-four and barely 100 pounds, our fourth president was the shortest and lightest chief executive in U.S. history and also the smallest of the founding fathers. By comparison, the average American man of his time was around five-foot-eight, although a number of the founding fathers were taller than average. Among them, Thomas Jefferson, our third president, was six-foot-two, and George Washington, our first president, was almost six-foot-one. Benjamin Franklin, the oldest of America's founding fathers, stood at nearly five-foot-eleven.

Little-known fact #2: Benjamin Franklin worked in the nude

We all enjoy fresh air, but Franklin took his enjoyment to extremes. The famous essayist, statesman, scientist, and inventor liked starting his day completely naked, with the window open. He called this ritual his "air bath." Even when it was too cold outside to open the window, he would sit in his room in his birthday suit and work, often writing official correspondence or crafting one of the many articles he wrote for publication. He sat naked for an hour or two before dressing and getting on with his day.

Little-known fact #3: John Adams thpoke with a lithp

Before the advent of modern dentistry, the most common treatment for a toothache was to have the offending tooth pulled—usually by a barber, whose job in those days included minor surgeries such as tooth-extraction. In the eighteenth century, it was not unusual for a person to be toothless by late middle age. By the time the sixty-four-year-old Adams took office as the second U.S. president in 1797, he had lost several teeth, including the front teeth necessary for making the "s" sound. He had a bridge of false teeth made but disliked wearing it, so he resigned himself to talking like Sylvester the Cat.

Little-known fact #4: George Washington was a dancing fool

He might look dour in paintings, but Washington was the life of the party. The general and statesman loved to cut a rug and was considered one of the best dancers in America. Dancing was a major part of social life in the eighteenth century, especially in Washington's native Virginia and the rest of the South. During the Revolutionary War, Washington and his officers fought wartime stress with parties centered on dancing and card playing. Dances—ranging from rigorously formal minuets to lively English country dances—were not considered intimate or even necessarily flirtatious. During his presidency, Washington toured all the states, and at many stops his hosts would throw balls in his honor, where local ladies would line up to dance with him.

Little-known fact #5: Thomas Jefferson pined for fine wine

Jefferson was a man of many passions. In addition to his day jobs writing the Declaration of Independence, serving as ambassador to France, and leading the nation as our third president, he was an architect, gardener, violinist, gourmet, inventor, and more. He loved fine wine and served as unofficial wine advisor to other presidents, including Washington. Jefferson planted vineyards on his Virginia estate, where the soil and climate were not ideal for the crop. Predictably, the resulting grapes and the wines they produced were no match for his favorite French varieties. In 1789, when he returned to America from Paris after five years as the U.S. ambassador to France, Jefferson brought back so much wine that he went into debt to pay for it.

Little-known fact #6: Patrick Henry worked dead-end jobs

Haven't decided on a career? Don't worry, even Patrick Henry got off to a slow start. The great Virginia orator—author of the famous phrase "give me liberty or give me death"—worked a number of dead-end jobs before he discovered his true calling. As a teenager, he worked in a general merchandise shop, but he tended to neglect the hard work of stocking shelves and ordering goods, which made him a poor shopkeeper. Next, he tried his hand at farming, but he found country life tedious, so he sold his land and slaves and used the money to buy another store. Unfortunately, he mismanaged his new business into failure within three years. Finally, well into his twenties, he became interested in the law. In courtroom speeches, the young lawyer developed the eloquent, passionate style of speaking that helped him win the election to Virginia's colonial legislature.

Little-known fact #7: Thomas Paine was no Rockefeller

Despite achieving great success as an author and political philosopher, Thomas Paine—who wrote the important revolutionary pamphlet *Common Sense*—fell repeatedly into poverty throughout his life. Born in England, Paine first failed at the underwear trade when he tried to follow in his father's footsteps as a corset maker. After moving to Philadelphia, he achieved success as a writer, but the idealistic Paine refused to accept payment so that his pamphlets could remain inexpensive. During the Revolutionary War, he held a clerical job with Congress but was forced to resign in 1779 after he leaked classified information in a well-meant attempt to expose corruption. At the end of the war, he found himself penniless once again. This pattern continued through the rest of his life until he died a poor man living in a rented room in New York City's Greenwich Village.

Chapter Three

The small embers that had landed on the roof above the stoop hadn't died out. They'd matured into a sizeable flame, and still nobody seemed to notice.

Except the time travelers. Mindy rushed forward, pointing at the flames above Widow Madison's head. "Fire! Your house is on fire!"

Widow Madison followed Mindy's wild gestures. "Raise the alarm!" she cried, but Samuel was already hurtling down the cobblestone street.

Suddenly a hand yanked Mindy backward. Using the moves she'd learned in the self-defense class her mom made her take one summer at the YMCA, she slammed her elbow into her attacker's stomach while simultaneously stomping his toe.

He released her, howling in pain. Mindy turned to face him but found only Jasper, doubled over and clutching his stomach.

"I'm so sorry!" Mindy said, crouching to look into his hazel eyes. "I didn't know it was you. Are you okay?"

Jasper nodded and thrust the chronolyzer into her hand. "Sure and I was only trying to show you this."

As Mindy read the glowing screen, her face numbed.

Target Alien: Glitta. Target Teenager: Serena Gold.

"Are you sure?" Mindy asked the chronolyzer.

Statistical probability is 100 percent.

Mindy's legs gave way beneath her, and as she started to crumple to the cobblestones, Jonathan caught her. "What's wrong?" he asked.

"It's my sister. The chronolyzer says my sister Serena is here." Mindy couldn't believe it. They'd finally found her—well almost. Mindy had gone through so much searching for her fifteen-year-old sister. She'd almost been hung as a witch searching for Serena in 1692 Salem. She'd had to dodge minie balls during the Battle of Bull Run to search for her during the Civil War. Now all she had to do was find her inside a burning building or an angry mob. She didn't care what it took—no matter what, she was going to find her sister and send her back home, and she certainly wasn't going to let some stupid colonial fire get in her way.

"We've got to put that fire out," Mindy said.

All around the time travelers, the crowd that had been so intent on thwarting the older woman just moments before had mobilized. The two burly men restraining Thomas released him. Others raced into their homes, returning with leather buckets and every spare person they could find. Even people who hadn't been involved in the unpleasantness came out to help fight the fire.

The Philadelphians formed two lines to transport buckets of water from some unseen source. One line passed full buckets toward the fire, and the other passed empty buckets back toward the water source.

Widow Madison returned from the boardinghouse with two leather buckets in each hand. A sharp girl with dark hair and eyes followed with a confident swagger.

"Hurry up, Bridget," Widow Madison said, taking a spot in the empty-bucket line.

The dark-haired Bridget slid in between the men.

Off in the distance a bell tolled, sounding what Mindy hoped might be Samuel's fire alarm.

Mindy slid the chronolyzer into the pocket beneath the folds in her gown and petticoats and took a spot in the bucket brigade with Jonathan and Jasper. The water arrived quickly, and it amazed Mindy how enemies could rally together in the face of adversity. That certainly hadn't been the case with her and Serena. Their parents' divorce five years ago might not have been as life-threatening as a fire, but it had been just as devastating.

To make ends meet, their mom had stepped up her hours at the souvenir shop and left Mindy in charge of her little sister. Serena resented being told what to do by someone who was only two years older than she was, and Mindy resented having to be the responsible one at twelve years old. It was even worse now that Serena was a freshman at Salem High. They fought constantly. But at this moment, Mindy wished she could take back every mean thing she'd ever said in their infinite, meaningless fights.

Mindy redoubled her bucket-passing efforts, ignoring her sore arms and encouraging others around her to pick up the pace. She was going to find Serena.

A pregnant teenager with curly auburn hair and freckles that reminded her of Serena's tottered out of the boardinghouse on the arm of grizzled elderly man. When the girl helped the elderly man down the stairs instead of the other way around, Mindy realized he was blind.

"Mr. Winsley and I are here to help," the pregnant girl said to Widow Madison, helping the blind man find a place in the bucket brigade.

"Thank you, Sarah, but please be careful. You're too near your time of lying in and could harm the child."

"We'll be fine," Sarah said, stroking her protruding stomach.

Samuel, the well-muscled man who had stood up for Widow Madison on the stoop, returned with a ladder. The bucket brigade diverted water to the roof, and the fire sizzled, more steam than smoke. By the time the volunteer fire company rolled up with their hand-pumped fire truck, the bucket brigade had extinguished the fire.

The mob that less than ten minutes ago had been so eager to see Widow Madison's neighbor's things burn to the ground clapped each other on the back and let out a celebratory cheer.

"Your keen eyesight saved my boardinghouse," Widow Madison, wiping her hands on her dingy apron, said to Mindy.

Mindy mumbled something, uncomfortable with the praise.

Jasper stepped forward and smiled openly at Widow Madison. "My companions—Mindy and Jonathan—and I were on our way to New York City, but Philadelphia looks prosperous enough to provide jobs for three more able-bodied youths."

Samuel, ladder held casually beneath one arm as if it were made of feathers instead of oak, snorted. "Good luck with that. The Intolerable Acts have closed down the ports even more than they had been before. No imports from or exports to Britain means no work for stevedores like me or general laborers of any sort. There's little work to do, even for the willing."

The dark-haired tomboy Bridget, who had toted full buckets alongside the men, put her hand on her hip. "And even less work available for the unwilling."

The pregnant girl, Sarah, giggled as she eased down onto the front steps of the boardinghouse. "Well, around here, that's only Peyton."

Widow Madison scowled reprovingly. "Peyton's a good boy. He just needs to be given a chance." Her tone was uncharacteristically soft. She obviously had a soft spot for Peyton.

The tomboy leaned over to Mindy and whispered loudly, "All he's getting around here is a chance to sleep until noon."

"Bridget Nugent, shut it!" Widow Madison said.

The girl fell silent, but her grin didn't fade.

"Do you think we might stay at your boardinghouse?" Jasper asked. "We couldn't pay at first, but as soon as we get jobs, we can get straight with you."

Widow Madison rubbed her hands on her apron, scrutinizing every detail. Despite an urge to bolt, or at least to shift her feet, Mindy just stood there as Widow Madison inspected the three of them. Finally, she spoke. "You'd have to work like the others."

Jonathan said sincerely, "Proverbs 12:24. 'Work hard and become a leader. Be lazy and never succeed.'"

"Bible quoting won't impress me," Widow Madison said, "but hard work will."

"Sure and you can count on us for that," Jasper agreed with an easy smile.

"I may have a reputation for taking in hard-luck cases, but we all contribute to the boardinghouse in our own way. Besides helping around the house, you'll pick oakum, do piecework, spin, and anything else I can come up with that will earn us money for food and the other necessities of life."

"So you live in a commune?" Mindy said. She didn't think they had those until the 1960s.

"We live together to keep out of the almshouse, if that's what you mean. We're pretty full up, though," Widow Madison said.

Samuel spoke up. "The men can share my room."

Widow Madison shook her head. "That's a kind offer, Samuel, but the gentlemen can have Peyton's room, and Peyton can stay with you. After all, he wouldn't have a roof to stay under if it weren't for these three. The girl can stay with Sarah and Bridget."

Bridget snickered.

"That's enough."

Samuel ran his fingers through his wavy brown hair, now caked with soot and smelling of smoke. "If I'm not needed, I think I'll go take a look at the damage to our roof."

"Thank you, Samuel. That would be kind of you. Roust Peyton to help you make any repairs."

Bridget beamed. "*I'll* go roust Peyton."

"I think not," Widow Madison said. "You're to stay away from Peyton Lynch. And there's spinning to be done."

Bridget's smile faded. "Yes, ma'am. I'll go tend to my duties."

Off to the side, Conrad and other rebels dug through the pile of leather buckets to retrieve their contributions. Mr. Winsley, the elderly blind man, was running his fingertips across the pile, evidently searching the intricate crests and designs on the outside of each bucket for the ones belonging to Widow Madison.

"Out of our way, square toes," Conrad said.

"I'm searching for our buckets," Mr. Winsley said.

Conrad laughed. "You couldn't find a bucket if you needed to pee in it."

Mr. Winsley puffed up. "And you couldn't find a sense of duty and honor if your mother had sewn it into your fancy waistcoat, you blasted agitator!"

The *A* word caught the ear of several of the other rebels, including the two hulking henchmen who had held Thomas back during the bonfire. One of them cracked his knuckles. "Did you hear what he called us, Fleet?"

"Agitator, that's what, Henry," Fleet answered, folding his arms across his chest.

"King George is the agitator. King George started all this by drowning us in taxes and using the colonies without giving anything back."

Mr. Winsley spat at the sound of Henry's voice. "Without giving anything back? What do you consider the forts and soldiers dispatched to protect us against the French? We are royal subjects, and King George may not give us all we are due, but your arrogant, destructive, *agitating* ways are not the solution to our problems."

"Tory," Fleet growled. "He's no better than Thomas, and he's got a bigger mouth."

Henry nodded. "Yes. Seems this Tory would be better off *mute* than *blind*."

Mindy's stomach sank. If someone didn't do something, they were going to beat up this helpless old man.

Loyal to the Royals:

4 Reasons Why Many American Colonists Remained Loyal to British Rule

About 20 percent of the colonists living in eighteenth-century America sided with the British in the Revolutionary War. In the days before Posh and Becks, what could have prompted such fealty?

Reason #1: They considered themselves British

Most Americans in the eighteenth century proudly considered themselves British. For starters, many colonists actually came from England, while others traced their ancestry back to England and Scotland. These colonists accepted the widely held belief that Britain's king was appointed by God to rule them. Even some patriots who fought against the British in the Revolutionary War did so not to gain independence but because they longed to reform existing British rule. Prominent clergyman Samuel Seabury of Connecticut spoke for many when he wrote, "If I must be enslaved, let it be by a king at least, and not by a parcel of upstart lawless committeemen."

Reason #2: They thought it was crazy to challenge the British army

On the British side, there was a well-trained army, the world's mightiest navy, and legions of experienced officers. On the American side, there were raw recruits, ragtag militia units, the barest beginnings of a navy, and a commander-in-chief with limited experience. It's no wonder that many colonists had second thoughts about challenging the British! Ironically, one reason that America eventually won the war was that Britain, assuming a huge force of loyalist Americans would rise in its support, failed to commit sufficient resources to the war effort. Despite the considerable number of British-supporting Americans, no such force came to Britain's aid.

Reason #3: They were slaves who had been promised freedom

It sounds unlikely, but the British army gained the support of a large number of runaway American slaves. In 1775, the British governor of Virginia, John Murray (better known to history as the Earl of Dunmore), issued a proclamation inviting slaves whose masters were sympathetic to the revolutionary cause to abandon their masters and join the British army. In exchange for military service, Dunmore and his British backers promised the slaves their freedom. There's no hard count of how many slaves answered Dunmore's call, but some historians estimate that as many as 800 runaways were organized into the Royal Ethiopian Regiment, one of several all-black units to serve on the British side. After the war, Britain resettled about 4,000 loyalist blacks to the colony of Nova Scotia, where some of the former slaves' descendents still live to this day.

Reason #4: They wanted to keep their jobs

We all need to make a living somehow. In eighteenth-century America, a large number of colonists received their paychecks from the British government, working in positions such as tax collector, customs agent, and harbormaster. Many of these colonists remained loyal to the king, either in hopes of job security, out of principle, or from a combination of these two forces. Too bad for them: As the rebellions grew and British colonial governments ceased to exist, many lost their jobs anyway. The most famous of these loyal British employees? Founding father Ben Franklin's own son, William, who served as the British-appointed royal governor of New Jersey. The younger Franklin repeatedly refused to heed his father's many entreaties to join the patriot cause and eventually left for England, where he lived estranged from his father—and from his native America.

Chapter Four

Jonathan stepped between Mr. Winsley and the rebels. "You'll not touch this man. He's done nothing wrong."

"Is that so?" Conrad said. "Perhaps you share this man's beliefs?"

"My beliefs are my own," Jonathan said.

Jasper appeared at the minister's side. "Sure and if you ask me, they're none of your fecking business."

Sarah wriggled on the front step, unable to get back up. She frantically waved for help as if getting off the stoop was the most important thing in the world. Although Mindy hated abandoning Jonathan and Jasper, she caved, just long enough to help the pregnant girl up.

Sarah waddled over to Henry, resting her fingers on his arm to show him that she was near. "Let's go inside, Mr. Winsley. I'll come back in a bit and get our buckets when they're finished."

He pulled his arm away. "If we let these *patriots* have their way, there will be nothing left for any of us when they're finished."

Mindy had the feeling they weren't discussing fire buckets anymore.

Conrad's grin became a smirk. "Is that so, old man? Perhaps if you hate America so much you should leave. I understand Canada is nice this time of year."

"I fought in the French and Indian War while you were still crapping in your diapers. I'll not be exiled to a place—"

Sarah took his arm again. "Please, Mr. Winsley, let's go inside. I'm not feeling very well. The baby is kicking."

"I won't be quashed," Mr. Winsley said.

"I know. It's just—oh!" Sarah grabbed at her stomach.

Widow Madison shot Sarah a silent, disapproving look. Was the pregnant teen faking her distress?

Mr. Winsley softened. "You should go sit down a spell."

"That's what I'll do," Sarah said. "Good idea, Mr. Winsley. Can you help me inside?"

"Of course, of course," he said, offering her his arm.

Conrad snorted. "You should watch yourself, Widow Madison. Your boardinghouse has always been a refuge for the *lower sort,* but now it overflows with rogues and ruffians."

"At least my rogues and ruffians don't go around trying to beat up blind old men," Widow Madison said, turning and leading Mindy, Jonathan, and Jasper into the modest three-story brick boardinghouse.

Clean and well-kept, the entire house was maybe twenty feet wide by thirty-five feet long and a duplicate of the one next door. The main floor had a small sitting room in front of a kitchen with a fireplace that took up almost half of one of the walls.

"Mindy, your room is upstairs—the second on the right, and gentlemen, yours is directly across from the girls'. You may deposit your belongings and come to the kitchen for your tasks."

A single staircase led to the second-floor bedrooms. Like the house next door, four doors lined a narrow hallway. Mindy followed Jonathan and Jasper into their room, finally feeling like she could breathe again.

"This is going to be great," Mindy said. "Contained—"

"Where's my bastard chronolyzer?" Jasper interrupted.

Mindy fished it out from the pocket beneath the folds of her gown and handed it to him. "Man, Jasper, aren't you a bit old to still need your blanky?" She'd never seen him so uptight about the chronolyzer before.

"Sure and I need to check in," Jasper said, snatching it from her. He pushed his curly hair up off his forehead and buried his nose in the chronolyzer.

"As I was saying," Mindy continued, "this is going to be great. We've got a contained environment, a limited number of potential host bodies—all who seem pretty friendly and approachable—and communal meals that will be easy to dose with tempose. What more could we ask for?"

"Sure, sure . . . easy," Jasper said, fiddling with the chronolyzer.

"Is everything well, friend Jasper?" Jonathan asked. "You seem a bit distracted."

"Sure and I'm fine, thank you, Minister." Jasper rubbed the back of his neck distractedly.

Mindy sighed. "Jasper Gordon, you haven't heard a single word we've said, have you?" She snatched the chronolyzer from him.

The glowing screen immediately turned black.

Mindy wanted to scream.

"Give me that!" Jasper said.

"Not until you tell me what's wrong."

"Wrong? What could possibly be wrong?" Jasper asked. "We just almost got burnt to a crisp, fought a fire with archaic buckets the size of great rocks, and kept a grumpy little old man from getting beaten to a pulp. Forgive me for feeling a wee bit . . . frazzled."

"Touchy, aren't we?" Mindy had never seen anything get to the feisty little man like this.

"Sure and I'm only on probation, Gold."

"And that's news? You seem as though you're permanently on probation."

"Well, this time is different. My bastard boss is watching every move I make—every move we make. He says Salem and Bull Run were stupendous failures—"

"But we rescued Chad and sent him back to his own time," Mindy protested.

"But we didn't capture Andros. So now my supervisor's second-guessing everything I do and making me file remote reports."

"We're about to find my sister, and you decide to start following procedure? This is a lame time for you to suddenly choose to be responsible."

"Look, I'm the first to tell those chrono-people to sod off, but they can make life pretty difficult for us." Jasper said.

Mindy softened. "Okay already. We'll all be well-behaved little Time Stream Investigators—"

Jasper rolled his eyes. "Sure and *I'm* the only Time Stream Investigator here. If I recall correctly, the two of you are just tagalongs."

"Tagalongs? Is that what you'd consider the girl who saved your butt in Salem? Andros would have crushed your skull if your *tagalong* hadn't stopped him."

Jasper's voice dripped with venom. "Oh, and I'm so glad you only let the fecker give me *one* great bloody gash on the head."

"You're impossible," Mindy said, tossing her silky, thick brown hair.

"Widow Madison is waiting for us," Jasper said. He strode toward the door and paused at the entrance. "Coming?"

Mindy nodded, confused. She let Jasper storm down the narrow stairs ahead of them. When he was out of earshot, she whispered to

Jonathan, "What's up with him? I was just trying to say we'd do what he wanted and . . . " She felt tears well up.

Jonathan put his arm around her. "Forget him. He's just crazy," he said flatly.

Mindy did a double-take at the minister's twenty-first-century language and burst into gales of laughter.

"What is it?" Jonathan asked. "He is, isn't he?"

Mindy blotted at her eyes with her fingertips. "Yeah, definitely."

As they reached the bottom of the stairs, Jonathan muttered, "I will never, ever understand the fairer sex."

A large fireplace dominated the kitchen. Mindy would have only had to stoop slightly to stand inside it. An iron bar went from one side to the other. A large kettle hung from it. As cool as it was for May, the warehouse-sized fireplace made it pretty unbearable. Mindy's scalp prickled, and she felt faint.

Widow Madison sent a scowling Jasper and an amiable Jonathan for firewood—as if any of them could handle more heat. She handed Mindy a cleaver and a squishy turnip to cut. Lunch, it appeared, was going to be some kind of root vegetable and beef stew, as Widow Madison had started cutting hunks of some foul-smelling salted meat.

Perhaps the thing Mindy liked least about time-travel, after the almost-hangings and minie-ball injuries, was the way everyone was always eating huge hunks of animal flesh. Mindy had been a vegetarian since middle school. She loved animals with all her heart, and she couldn't understand anyone wanting to kill one just to eat it. She certainly couldn't eat one of her friends.

Oh well. She'd just have to eat around it.

Widow Madison lopped off another hunk of salted meat. "I'm thankful for your assistance," she said. "Sarah used to be a big help to me, but she's near her time of lying in, and the heat troubles her much."

"I'm thankful for the opportunity to help," Mindy said. "I'm happy to be in your home." As she chopped her turnip, she realized she was telling the truth.

When Widow Madison left the table to tend to the fire, Mindy put a little under half the vial of tempose into the soup pot. The host body would need to consume more than that for Mindy to be able to use the chronolyzer to send Serena back to her own time, but she'd learned the hard way that slower was better. During their last adventure she'd administered too much too quickly with disastrous results. She wouldn't make that mistake again. Since the host seemed likely to be staying within this house, she could just dose everyone's food.

Jasper and Jonathan returned with far too much firewood in their arms and set it on top of the previous stash next to the hearth. A twitchy nose, thin whiskers, and beady black eyes poked through the mound of wood.

"A mouse!" Mindy said.

Widow Madison remained unruffled. "I call him Mr. Double-Tripe because of the fat belly. He's good luck. If he's around, that means we don't have rats."

Mindy bent down for a closer look, and Jonathan joined her. Jasper folded his arms across his chest, remaining aloof. "He's cute," Jonathan said.

"Except Mr. Double-Tripe is a Mrs.," Mindy said. "She's got a good dozen hairless pink babies in a nest in here."

Widow Madison put her hands on her hips. "You don't say? Well, Mrs. Double-Tripe and her babies will need to find a new home outside. One mouse is good; a family of mice is not." She turned to Jonathan and Jasper. "Gentlemen, do you think you might be so kind as to convey the new mother and her babies to a safe spot in the woodshed?"

"Of course," Jonathan said.

A knock came from the front door.

"Mindy, could you please get that?" Widow Madison asked as she bent down to inspect the nest.

"Sure," Mindy said, scampering off through the parlor toward the front door. In the main room, Sarah ran a large spinning wheel while Bridget pulled long plant stalks through a wooden brush with metal bristles.

"Mr. Double-Tripe had babies!" Mindy said, running to the door. "In the woodpile next to the hearth!"

Sarah and Bridget abandoned their spinning and headed for the kitchen.

The knock repeated at the front door.

Mindy opened the door, her mind still on the twelve pink bundles in the woodpile.

On the stoop, a woman in her mid-twenties held a baby wrapped in a blanket. The woman's face was pitted and discolored with blotchy scars. She tottered weakly, as if she hadn't had anything to eat in days.

"Are you okay?" Mindy asked.

"It's not me. It's my baby. She's very sick."

"You should take her to the hospital." Mindy hoped she hadn't just said something stupid. Did Philadelphia even have a hospital in 1775?

"I don't have money for the hospital. I've no one to turn to. I understand Widow Madison helps people." Tears streamed down the woman's dirt-smudged cheeks. "Please, help my little girl!"

Revolution Revised:

7 Myths and Misperceptions About the Revolutionary War

Wooden teeth, midnight rides, and whites of their eyes? Well, sort of.

Myth #1: Paul Revere rode solo

Revere's famous midnight ride was not a solo act—nor was it a duo or even a trio. He was just one of a slew of riders who set out on the night of April 18, 1775, to warn American militia leaders of the advance of British troops. Revere was assigned to ride from Charlestown to Lexington, where John Adams and John Hancock were staying. Another patriot, William Dawes, was also assigned to ride to Lexington, albeit over a different route (the hope was that if one rider didn't make it, the other would). Luckily, both night riders made it to Lexington, America won the war, and the rest is history, right? Not so fast. After reaching Lexington, Revere and Dawes decided to ride together to Concord to warn additional militia leaders there. On this last leg of the journey, their luck ran out. The Brits caught Revere and confiscated his horse; Dawes gave pursuers the slip, but his horse bucked him off and ran away. Only a third rider they had picked up along the way, Samuel Prescott, made it to Concord. Stranded in the middle of the night without their horses, Revere and Dawes ended up journeying back to Lexington on foot.

Myth #2: The Battle of Bunker Hill took place on Bunker Hill

When American soldiers decided to build a fortification on a peninsula in Boston Harbor in June of 1775, they picked Breed's Hill over its neighbor, Bunker Hill. And Breed's Hill is where most of the fighting took place during the famous battle on June 16. For reasons lost to history, the first major battle of the Revolutionary War became known as the Battle of Bunker Hill—even though it took place on Breed's Hill.

Myth #3: American troops were rallied by the famous order, "Don't fire until you see the whites of their eyes."

It sure sounds nice, but there's no real historical evidence suggesting that these words were spoken at the Battle of Bunker Hill. The story is a familiar one: Low on ammunition, the scrappy American troops found themselves heavily outnumbered by ranks of spiffy, well-armed Redcoats. General Israel Putnam, leader of the American troops, sized up the situation and gave his famous order, implying that his men should be patient and make every shot count. Veterans of the fight, however, differed in their opinions about which of several officers present issued the order and just what was said. Some remembered the command as, "Do not fire until you see the *color* of their eyes." Boston newspapers credited Putnam with the now familiar wording, and he has gone down in history as the author of the memorable line.

Myth #4: The Liberty Bell rang on July 4

Many of us learned—or maybe we just *think* we learned—that the Liberty Bell rang on July 4, 1776. The truth is, the famous bell in the tower of the Pennsylvania State House (later renamed Independence Hall) rang four days later, on July 8, 1776. The occasion? A celebration of the first public reading of the Declaration of Independence, which had been approved by the Second Continental Congress four days earlier.

Myth #5: John Hancock signed big to taunt England's King George III

Legend has it that Hancock signed the Declaration of Independence with a flourish and said, "King George will be able to read that without spectacles. He may now double the reward for my head." It makes a good story, but in all likelihood, Hancock was just signing in his usual grand fashion. As president of the Second Continental Congress, the body that drew up and approved the Declaration, Hancock had an outsized position reflected in his outsized signature. He signed the Declaration on July 4, 1776, nearly a month before other members of Congress added their signatures on August 2.

Myth #6: George Washington wore a set of wooden teeth

Wooden teeth for a man of Washington's stature? Pshaw! A rich man, Washington ordered the best dentures that money could buy. He owned several sets of choppers crafted mostly from ivory and hippopotamus teeth, sometimes assembled in combination with real human teeth (barbers, who were also in the business of tooth-pulling in the eighteenth century, frequently sold harvested teeth to denture makers). Back in the day, the teeth would be fitted with gold springs that looped inside the person's cheeks to hold them firmly against the gums. Be grateful for the wonders of modern dentistry: By the time you're old enough to be president, chances are you'll still have your own healthy incisors and molars.

Myth #7: George Washington was the first U.S. president

Okay, we know this is a stretch, but—due to a technicality—Washington was *not* the first U.S. president. That honor (technically) goes to Maryland plantation owner John Hanson, who was given the title "President of the United States in Congress Assembled" when his fellow delegates elected him president of Congress in 1781. But Washington wasn't the second, third, fourth, fifth, sixth, seventh, or even *eighth* president, either. Eight other presidents of Congress followed Hanson until the new U.S. Constitution created the modern position of president as chief executive.

Chapter Five

Sticky, oozing sores covered the child from head to toe. Even the palms of her hands and the bottoms of her feet were covered in the sores. The little girl's eyes were almost swollen shut with the pustules.

"I . . . I don't . . ." Mindy stammered. She'd never seen anyone that sick, ever. "I have to check with—"

Widow Madison bustled to the door, wiping her hands on her white apron. "Mindy, don't be rude. We don't leave visitors out on the stoop. Let them in."

When Widow Madison saw the seeping, blister-covered baby, her gray eyes darkened. "No, not again—"

The woman on the doorstep cocked her head and grinned crookedly. The look sent chills through Mindy. It was the same smug look Andros had given her when he'd possessed Jonathan at the Battle of Bull Run and made him shoot an innocent boy. It was the same irritatingly pleased look he always had whenever he possessed a human host and made it do unspeakable things against its will. It didn't matter who he inhabited—bewitched teenage girls, constables, or Confederate soldiers, Andros's menacing, self-satisfied grin always revealed him.

Suddenly the woman's eyes rolled back in her head, and she crumpled onto the stoop on top of the child. The little girl squealed.

Without thinking, Mindy rushed out and rolled the mother off of the toddler.

"Don't touch it!" Widow Madison cried. "It's the pox!"

The mother woke up disoriented. "Where am I?" When she saw Mindy holding her little girl, she shrieked, "Give me my baby!"

Mindy shoved the toddler, still partially wrapped in its blanket, back at her mother just as Jonathan, Jasper, Sarah, and Bridget arrived at the door, drawn by the commotion.

"Everyone inside," Mindy said. "Now!" When Andros left a body, the host crumpled just like the mother had. If it was indeed Andros and not just the disease, Andros could hop into any of the boarders at any second.

The tone in Mindy's voice conveyed her seriousness. Everyone backed up, and just as Mindy was about to close the door, a disheveled yet handsome young man about Samuel's age strolled up the steps wearing a shirt of white homespun linen, a lead-gray vest, and trousers instead of breeches.

"What's all this?" he said, slouching. He reeked of stale rum.

"Get inside, Peyton," Widow Madison said.

He ambled inside.

Widow Madison turned to the woman on the doorstep. "Go back to your own home. Do not spread your foul diseases here."

The woman clutched her child to her chest and shook her head. "I'm sorry. I don't know what came over me . . . "

Widow Madison slammed the door in her face. "If the pox has returned to Philadelphia, we're only safe inside."

"Fine if you want to stay in, but you're not keeping *me* here," Peyton said. "I've got places to go, people to see."

Bridget murmured, "And ale to drink, I expect."

Widow Madison shook and broke out in a sweat. "No one is leaving," she said, her voice quavering.

"I'll do what I want," Peyton said. It's not like Philadelphia hasn't had the pox before. Either you get it, or you don't. There's nothing you can do about it."

Jonathan nodded. "It's a decision to be put in God's hands."

"My Inner Light says God helps them that help themselves. Until we know how wide-spread the pox is, no one leaves. Do I make myself clear?" Widow Madison glared at Peyton.

Peyton folded his arms across his chest but didn't respond.

"If you want to sleep on the streets with the pox-mongers, be my guest." She waved her hand toward the door.

Peyton's lips formed a thin line. "Fine."

"I need to think this through," Widow Madison said, "figure things out. Everyone to their rooms."

The docile group filed up the stairs. On the landing, Mindy grabbed Jasper. "We need to talk."

"Right," he said. "Now."

Mindy followed him and Jonathan into their room.

The minute the door closed, Jasper bristled. "How could you be so daft? You just exposed us all to smallpox!"

"What was I supposed to do, let the baby get smothered underneath the mother when she fell?"

"Your intentions were admirable," Jonathan said, "but that child clearly has an appointment with God."

"What?"

Jasper threw his hands up. "Sure and he means she's going to die! Smallpox is *extremely* contagious, and it is almost always fatal for babies."

Mindy thought about the baby girl, and tears welled up in her eyes. "The poor thing . . . "

"Poor thing? Poor us!" Jasper said.

"Isn't there a cure or a vaccination or something? Nobody in the twenty-first century gets smallpox anymore."

Jasper pulled the chronolyzer from his suit coat. "Chronolyzer, we all may have been infected with smallpox. What are our treatment options?"

THE DATE IS MAY 9, 1775, THE DAY BEFORE THE SECOND CONTINENTAL CONGRESS CONVENES AT THE STATE HOUSE HERE IN PHILADELPHIA. IF WE WERE JUST A SCANT TWENTY-FIVE YEARS IN THE FUTURE, THIS WHOLE MESS COULD HAVE BEEN AVOIDED. EDWARD JENNER'S VACCINATION CREATED FROM THE MILDER COW-POX INFECTION WOULD BE AVAILABLE ACROSS THE COLONIES, THANKS TO BENJAMIN WATERHOUSE, WHO BROUGHT THE PROCEDURE ACROSS THE POND. JENNER'S VAC-CINATION WILL SIGNIFICANTLY REDUCE THE INCIDENCES OF SMALLPOX. IF THIS WERE 1800, YOU PROBABLY WOULD HAVE NEVER BEEN INFECTED.

"Sure and we're very grateful for the medical history lesson, in spite of its total irrelevance. But since we may have already been infected," Jasper said, "what would you be suggesting we do now?"

YOUR OPTIONS ARE LIMITED. OF COURSE, BEING CARBON-BASED, AREN'T THEY ALWAYS?

Mindy ignored the chronolyzer's jab. There was no time for another spat.

THE MOST COMMON KIND OF PREVENTIVE MEASURE FOR SMALLPOX IS SOME-THING CALLED VARIOLATION. IT IS A PROCEDURE ADMINISTERED BY DOCTORS, AND I USE THAT TERM LOOSELY, AT INOCULATION HOSPITALS. BASICALLY YOU—

"Wait a second," Mindy said. "Why are we even discussing options for 1775? Jasper, why don't you just pop on back to 2512 and get the cure? I mean, you can cure smallpox in 2512, right?"

"Yes, but that's not going to be an option. I can't bring anything from the future back to the past, at least nothing that's going to change history."

"Why not? When we were at the Battle of Bull Run during our last trip, and the host body got his leg shot, you went back to 2512 and brought that funky surgical bandage—"

"The auto-surgeon strip," Jasper corrected.

"The point is, it totally repaired the wound, and without it, Alexander would have had his leg amputated."

Jasper ran his fingers through his hair. "It's complicated, Mindy. As a Time Stream Investigator, they expect me to ensure the stability of the time stream, not change events. When someone like Andros gets loose in the time stream, my responsibility is to make sure he doesn't mess things up. That's what he did in the Civil War episode. That Alexander would have never been shot if Andros's buddy Remez hadn't possessed him. All I did was put things back the way they were supposed to be."

"How do you know that was what you were doing? There's nothing that says he wouldn't have been shot anyhow."

"Any decision of this kind involves a complex algorithm that the chronolyzer—"

"Complex algorithms? Everyone in this house might be at risk, and you're talking about math calculations?"

"I wasn't the one who put them at risk, Mindy Gold," he looked at her meaningfully.

"So if I put them at risk, we have to put them back the way we found them, right?"

"Time Stream Investigators don't normally go about making a holy show of themselves and mucking up the time stream. My authorization is strictly limited to correcting alien mistakes. If I tell my boss you botched it, *I'm* the one who's going to be in trouble."

"So don't tell him."

"That would never fly."

"So wait—you're suddenly deciding to be a by-the-book kind of guy now that we're in an emergency? That makes no sense. I mean, Mrs. Double-Tripe has more guts than you. Take some risks."

Jonathan cocked his head and rubbed his square jaw. "It seems to me that we don't yet know if Mindy opening the door to a stranger actually infected the house. We don't know if any damage has been done to the time stream. Perhaps repairs aren't necessary."

Mindy beamed. "He's right! Run your precious algorithms and see."

Jasper looked down at the dull pewter buckles on his thick leather shoes and coughed. "Em. I would, but there's a problem."

Founding Mothers:

9 Revolutionary Women in Eighteenth-Century America

Woman #1, the female Paul Revere: Sybil Ludington (1761–1839)

On the night of April 26, 1777, volunteer militia commander Colonel Henry Ludington learned that British troops had set fire to Danbury, Connecticut, twenty-five miles from where he lived in what is now Kent, New York. Sybil, Ludington's sixteen-year-old daughter, volunteered to alert the soldiers scattered all over the countryside with their families. From about nine that night until sunrise the next morning, she rode from house to house calling to the militiamen. It was too late to save Danbury, but—thanks in part to Sybil's bravery—the militiamen gathered in time to face the British and drive them south toward Long Island Sound.

Woman #2, the original Yentl: Deborah Samson (1760–1827)

In the spring of 1782, Deborah Samson joined the 4th Massachusetts Regiment, using the name Robert Shurtleff. At five-foot-seven, she was taller than the average woman of the time and quite strong. She served in several skirmishes and was wounded in the head and thigh that July. After the military doctor had cleaned and bandaged a cut on her head, she slipped out of the hospital before he could tend to the leg because she was afraid he would discover her secret. Using a penknife and a sewing needle, she dug a musket ball out of her thigh. After receiving an honorable discharge in 1783, Samson married and had three daughters. Later in her life, she petitioned for, and eventually received, recognition and military pension pay from both the Massachusetts and federal governments.

Woman #3, the cannon shooter: Margaret Corbin (1751–1800)

Margaret Corbin was wounded in action while single-handedly operating a cannon in defense of Fort Washington, an American garrison on the high ground at the northern tip of Manhattan Island. On November 16, 1776, a force of 6,000 to 8,000 Hessian soldiers (German mercenaries fighting for the British) attacked the fort. Outnumbered, the American force of about 3,000 defended the position, which was strategically important because it overlooked the Hudson River. Margaret Corbin joined her husband, John, in a two-person team operating one of the fort's cannons. After he was killed by enemy fire, she continued to fire the cannon until she was seriously wounded. Widely hailed for her courage, she is buried in West Point Cemetery.

Woman #4, the great Molly Pitcher: Mary Hayes (c.1753–1832)

At the battle of Monmouth in 1778, Mary was helping the American artillerymen, including her husband, William, by bringing them pitchers of water to swab out their cannons. It was a blazing hot day at the end of June, so the men also were pouring some of the water over themselves to avoid heatstroke. When William Hayes fell wounded, his wife took over his cannon and continued firing. Legend has it that after the battle, George Washington made her a sergeant, although if he did it was surely a symbolic gesture. The name "Molly Pitcher" may have been a general term for women who carried water for artillerymen, but the legend of a fighting Molly Pitcher seems to have originated with Mary Hayes.

Woman #5, the drama queen: Mercy Otis Warren (1728–1814)

In her 1772 play *The Adulateur*, playwright, essayist, and pamphleteer Mercy Otis Warren of Plymouth, Massachusetts, mocked contemporary Boston political figures, especially the British lieutenant governor of Massachusetts. Although she also poked fun at revolutionary leaders, Warren was an influential voice for independence. After the war, she wrote poetry, history, and newspaper pieces opposing the ratification of the U.S. Constitution. Warren thought power should rest with the individual states rather than with a central government.

Woman #6, the original abolitionist: Phyllis Wheatley (c.1753–1784)

Born in either Senegal or Gambia, Phyllis Wheatley was about eight years old when a Boston family bought her as a house slave. Realizing how intelligent she was, the family gave Phyllis the same education that they gave their own children. She became an accomplished poet. Her popularity helped earn her freedom in 1773, and she became a supporter of the independence movement. Wheatley tried to use both her celebrity and her poetry to convince revolutionary leaders that their cause was sullied by the institution of slavery. Although she did not succeed in her lifetime, she helped build support for the eventual abolition of slavery.

Woman #7, the trusted advisor: Abigail Adams (1744-1818)

While he was attending to the business of revolution in Philadelphia, John Adams corresponded regularly with his wife, Abigail, in Massachusetts. The letters demonstrate Mrs. Adams's intelligence and her husband's willingness to take her council. As Adams consulted with Jefferson and Franklin on the Declaration of Independence, she advised him to "remember the ladies and be more generous and favourable to them than your ancestors." It's unlikely that she was arguing for the vote for women, a concept unheard of at the time, but she was a strong advocate of education and broader opportunities for women. Abigail Adams later made a mark as a gracious First Lady, the first to live in the still-unfinished White House.

Woman #8, the first of the First Ladies: Martha Washington (1731-1802)

During the Revolutionary War, Martha Washington did not stay home at Mount Vernon while her husband, George, was with his troops. She frequently joined him for months at a time at his military quarters. Although she loved throwing elaborate parties at Mount Vernon and would do so again during her husband's presidential administration, she adopted a wartime policy of simple living to set an example for the other officers' wives. But while careful to economize, she also organized entertainments for the troops to boost morale.

Woman #9, the woman with the flag: Betsy Ross (c. 1703–1783)

Maybe she did. Maybe she didn't. No one really knows. The story of Betsy Ross sewing the first American flag grew from a family legend that her grandson shared with the world many years after Elizabeth Griscom Ross died. There are no hard facts—no invoices, no records—to substantiate his claim that she sewed the first flag. But Ross did run an upholstery shop in her home near the Pennsylvania State House, she did take jobs as a seamstress, and she did make flags—as evidenced by an order for flags she sewed for the Pennsylvania navy. Further, George Ross, a Pennsylvania delegate to the Second Continental Congress, was the uncle of her late husband. Assuming Ross did good work and was trustworthy, it seems likely that George Ross would have steered a bit of business to his niece-in-law. Regardless of who sewed the first flag with the stars and stripes design, it was probably a woman, and that woman deserves to be honored. Whoever she was, we'll call her Betsy Ross.

Chapter Six

Mindy frowned. "What kind of problem?"

Jasper didn't look up. "When I made the chronolyzer enhancement that allowed us to narrow the search field, there wasn't enough storage space to upload it. I had to strip the chronolyzer of a few minor programs—"

I FEEL SO DIRTY, the chronolyzer typed. SO USED.

"Jasper, you didn't."

"I mean, how many times did we use the Historical Accuracy Monitor function when we were at Bull Run? Of all the chronolyzer's components, I thought we'd miss the HAM program least . . . "

Jonathan said, "You could travel back to 2512 and do the calculations. If the result indicates that no one is infected, our problem is solved."

"But what if *everyone* is infected?" Mindy insisted. "You'll have to bring back a cure."

Jasper shook his head. "Not unless the HAM levels are high. Not unless something one of us has done has messed with the time stream."

"So if everyone is infected, we just wait for all of them to die?"

"With the chronolyzer enhancement, we know that your sister is inside of one of the boarders. It shouldn't take long to figure out which one and dose him or her appropriately. We'll be out of here before the seven- to ten-day incubation period."

"In the history of the world, there can't have been anyone more maliciously indifferent to human suffering than you are at this very minute!"

The chronolyzer began a list. NERO, HITLER, BOB BARKER . . .

Mindy asked, "It won't bother you at all to see all these innocent people die of smallpox, will it?"

"Sure and everyone dies, Mindy. You don't go traveling through time trying to stop the folks you see from dying. That makes no sense at all if you stop to think about it."

Mindy wanted to chuck Jasper out the window.

As always, Jonathan played the peacemaker. "Let us apply our reason to this problem and break it down into steps. The first step is simply for Jasper to run the calculations in 2512 to see if corrections must be made. Do we agree on that?"

Mindy nodded.

Jasper shrugged, "Sure and I suppose so."

"So what is step two, then?" Jonathan continued. "If the chronolyzer says we're all infected, and it's our fault, then Jasper can obtain authorization to bring back a cure. Isn't that correct?"

Jasper nodded tentatively. "Sure and *if* it was our fault."

"Agreed."

"But what if it wasn't our fault?" Mindy insisted. "Are we going to just let everyone die?"

"Now, Moses did not part the Red Sea until he needed to, Mindy." Jonathan's green eyes sparkled.

Jasper laughed. "In other words, we'll just deal with that problem later on?"

"Exactly."

"Fine, then I'll be leaving you now," Jasper said.

He handed Mindy the chronolyzer. "You'll need this."

Mindy felt unexpectedly pleased that he'd given the chronolyzer to her instead of Jonathan. "But how are you going to get around without it?" Mindy asked.

"I'll show you how to transport me from here, and I'll come back with a replacement."

AS LONG AS IT'S NOT A TWENTY-FIRST-CENTURY CALCULATOR, the chronolyzer typed.

"Or an abacus," Mindy joked, holding the device with a new respect. Until now she'd used it only as an interactive encyclopedia, not as a tool to zap someone through time and space.

"It's perfectly simple," Jasper said. "You just set the coordinates, then press this button, and this one, and do a few more quick calculations—"

OR YOU CAN JUST LET ME SET THE COORDINATES AND DO THE CALCULATIONS AND THEN YOU PRESS THE GREEN BUTTON TWICE, the chronolyzer typed.

"And whatever you do, don't press that red button labeled *PANIC* unless I'm dead—or you are."

"I'm not pressing any button once I'm dead."

"My point exactly," Jasper said. "Don't press the red button."

"I'm sure we'll be okay," Mindy said. "Just come back soon, okay?"

"Now you know, Mindy girl," Jasper said, grinning as he shrugged, "it's time travel. You'll barely know I'm gone. Now press that button."

In a flash of white light, Jasper disappeared.

Jonathan stood stiffly in the middle of the room without making eye contact with Mindy. It had been a long time since they had been alone together.

"You should get back to your room," Jonathan said without looking up. "I'll ensure no one knows Jasper is gone."

"Come and get me as soon as he returns, okay?"

"Absolutely. And Mindy," Jonathan said, looking up, "Be careful, will you? We may not be in jail or on a battlefield, but there are still dangerous things around. Andros might be here, or his alien cohort may wake up in the host body and start controlling it, or—"

Mindy grinned. "So now that Jasper's gone you think it's your job to lecture me?"

Minister Hartthorne reddened. "I didn't mean to imply that you were anything but fully capable. In fact, you're the most capable woman—no, *person*—I've ever met. I just meant—"

"It's okay," Mindy said, leaning toward him. "I think it's cute." Before she realized what she was doing, she kissed him on the cheek. Her lips barely brushed his strong, square jaw, but she felt his warmth travel across her face.

"Mindy—"

She dashed out of Jonathan's room and into Sarah and Bridget's, trying not to look like she'd just kissed a guy who would have been graduating high school when she was still in middle school—if he hadn't already been dead for over three hundred years.

"Where have you been, Mindy?" Sarah asked. The pregnant girl looked genuinely concerned.

"I needed to talk to my friends," Mindy said truthfully. "None of us has had smallpox, and we're all very worried." Jasper had taught her the best way to fake your way through unfamiliar time periods was to tell the truth—just not all of it.

"Really?" Bridget asked. "Does *talking* to your gentlemen always leave you breathless and blushing?"

"Bridget! We shouldn't pry into her matters."

"They're our matters too—when she's staying in our room."

"Widow Madison will indeed have a fit if she finds out you disobeyed her," Sarah said.

"I won't do it again," Mindy said.

The small room would have been cramped with only one person, but with three people in it, there wasn't much room for anything. At least she'd have the opportunity to interview two of the boarders at the same time to see if Serena was inside one of them. It usually took a while for a spirit to awaken in a host body. Once they did, they didn't always express themselves right away because it took a while to come to grips with waking up in someone else's body several hundred years in the past. Or so it seemed to Mindy.

"Well, we'd better make the most of our time," Sarah said. "We'll pick oakum. There's some under the bed—"

Bridget groaned. "My fingers are raw from the last batch."

Mindy wondered what kind of plant could make your fingers raw and why it would be growing in complete darkness beneath the bed. She had some ideas for twenty-first-century plants, but eighteenth-century flora was a different matter.

Sarah ignored Bridget's complaint. "Mindy, I can't exactly crawl under the bed with this stomach of mine. Could you reach under there for me?"

"Okay," Mindy said. As she bent down on her hands and knees, she suddenly wondered if oakum was some kind of animal and whether you had to pick fleas off of it or something. Maybe it had fangs and germy saliva that could cause diseases worse than smallpox.

Steeling herself, Mindy reached her hand into the darkened space beneath the bed.

Revolutionary Countdown:

10 People Who Rocked the American Revolution

They had time to invent, publish, speechify, and found a nation. Ah, the productivity that was possible in the days before Facebook and Wikipedia!

#10: Gouverneur Morris (1752–1816)

Although he's perhaps most famous for writing the final draft of the U.S. Constitution and its iconic preamble—"We, the people of the United States"—Morris's achievements go far beyond his flair for words. Morris was a lawyer, financial expert, Pennsylvania congressman and, later, a U.S. Senator. As a member of the 1777 Continental Congress, he shrewdly recognized that Washington's army was in dire shape and procured desperately needed supplies and pay for the soldiers in the winter of that year. He also served as the assistant finance minister under the Articles of Confederation, where he devised the decimal system for U.S. currency. On top of all that, he was reportedly also a lovely dancer, an impressive feat for a gentleman whose carriage accident at age twenty-eight had left him with one wooden leg.

#9: Benjamin Franklin (1706–1790)

Franklin was a Philadelphia printer, publisher, author, inventor, scientist, activist, diplomat, and humorist—in other words, an all-around colonial dynamo. After living in England for most of the fifteen years prior to the Revolution, Franklin returned to America and roused suspicion among some colonists: He'd been in London so long they feared he'd defected to the Brits and was working as a spy. However, his work as a colonial representative in England was a driving force behind the eventual repeal of the Stamp Act in 1766, securing his legacy as America's number-one patriot. As the elder statesman (literally) among the founding fathers, he brought his stature as an internationally famous scientist and philosopher to the Second Continental Congress of 1775. Franklin, a bona fide Renaissance man, is credited with establishing the first public library, wooing the French for support in the Revolutionary War, and inventing various notable gadgets, including bifocals, the urinary catheter, and scuba flippers.

#8: Patrick Henry (1736–1799)

A lawyer, politician, and brilliant orator, Henry used his gift for public speaking to rally his fellow Virginians to the cause of independence and became the first governor of Virginia in 1776. At the second Virginia Convention—a 1775 assembly to address the growing conflict with the British—Henry argued powerfully in favor of equipping the Virginia Militia for the armed struggle ahead. In this, his most famous speech, he cried out to his fellow delegates, "I know not what course others may take, but as for me, give me liberty or give me death!" After the war, Henry remained fearful of giving the federal government too much power and actually opposed the adoption of the U.S. Constitution. He changed his mind only after the addition of the Bill of Rights.

#7: Thomas Paine (1737–1809)

Paine was an English-born political radical, writer, and influential pamphleteer who moved to America on the advice of Benjamin Franklin, an acquaintance he'd met in London in 1774. Paine's fifty-page pamphlet *Common Sense,* published on January 10, 1776, sold more than 500,000 copies in the first half of that year—the months leading up to the Declaration of Independence. The pamphlet's eloquent and passionate argument for revolution against the Brits had a powerful effect on colonial public opinion, probably more powerful than that of any other single publication. The following winter, General Washington distributed Paine's next series of pamphlets, *The American Crisis,* to his dispirited troops. Beginning with the famous line, "These are the times that try men's souls," *Crisis* reinvigorated colonial morale and became a rallying cry for the revolution.

#6: The Marquis de La Fayette (1757–1834)

With a name like Marie-Joseph-Paul-Yves-Roch-Gilbert Du Motier, Marquis de La Fayette, it's no wonder he opted for the abbreviated version. A French nobleman, La Fayette traveled to America in 1777 to take up the revolutionary cause and became an effective general of the Continental Army. After serving with distinction under Washington in 1777–1778, La Fayette returned to France, where he helped persuade King Louis XVI to send 6,000 troops to help the Americans—a huge boost to the revolution. Then La Fayette sailed for America again, where units under his command pinned down British general Charles Cornwallis at Yorktown, Virginia, leading to the Brits' surrender on October 19, 1781.

#5: Alexander Hamilton (c. 1755–1804)

A lawyer, an Army officer, a politician, and a political essayist, Hamilton became the first U.S. secretary of the treasury in 1789. He was a powerful advocate for a strong central U.S. government and the chief author of the *Federalist Papers*, a series of influential essays—co-written by James Madison and John Jay—that played a major role in the shaping and ratifying of the U.S. Constitution. Later, as secretary of the treasury, Hamilton helped develop the U.S. economy by establishing the first national bank and an import tax system. Ona separate note, the Hamilton family was a cantankerous bunch: Philip, Alexander's son, was killed in a duel in 1801, three years before his father also fell to his death on that very same spot in his legendary duel with Vice President Aaron Burr.

#4: John Adams (1735–1826)

Adams was the first vice president of the United States, the second president, and the first to actually live in the White House. Originally a Boston lawyer and essayist, Adams was one of the earliest delegates to the First Continental Congress to argue for independence from Britain. His 1775 essays on the topic, published under the title *Novanglus*, helped turn public opinion toward revolution and won Adams a reputation as the "Colossus of Independence." In the Second Continental Congress, Adams selected Jefferson to write the Declaration of Independence and nominated Washington as commander of the Continental Army.

#3: James Madison (1751–1836)

At the Constitutional Convention in 1789, Madison, a student of history and the theory of government, played such a prominent role in shaping the U.S. Constitution that he's now remembered as the "Father of the Constitution." In addition to co-authoring the *Federalist Papers* with Alexander Hamilton and John Jay, Madison was also the sponsor of the Bill of Rights, created to protect the rights of citizens and check the federal government's power. Despite his achievements, Madison was a pretty bashful fellow. Luckily, his fun-loving wife, Dolley Payne Todd Madison, had enough personality for the both of them. Dolley was a beloved fixture in the Washington social scene and in the White House, where she hosted lavish parties for political leaders and average citizens alike.

#2: Thomas Jefferson (1743–1826)

Jefferson, another Renaissance man in the vein of Leonardo da Vinci and Ben Franklin, was a planter, lawyer, writer, and the governor of Virginia during the Revolution. As a Virginia delegate to the Second Continental Congress, Jefferson was the main author of the Declaration of Independence, which brilliantly and eloquently stated the causes for the American Revolution. A famous Francophile, he relocated to the Champs Elysees in Paris after the war, working as U.S. ambassador to France before returning stateside to serve in Washington's cabinet. Later, when he was president, Jefferson vastly increased the size of the new nation with his purchase of the Louisiana Territory from France. He also commissioned the Lewis and Clarke expedition to the Pacific Ocean, setting the precedent for a nation that stretched from sea to sea.

#1: George Washington (1732–1799)

This one's a no-brainer. As everyone knows, Washington's likeness appears on the quarter, the dollar bill, and the side of a mountain—not too shabby for a Virginia-born planter. After getting his big break in the French and Indian War and learning as he went along, Washington mastered the craft of warfare during the Revolution, securing victory and independence for the new nation in 1781. Later in that decade, he lent his influential support to the drafting and adopting of the U.S. Constitution and served as president of the Constitutional Convention. As the first U.S. president under that constitution, he set the precedent for the restrained exercise of executive power. He also retired after his second term in office, setting the American example of a peaceful and lawful transfer of power from one presidential administration to the next.

Chapter Seven

If she died of a vicious oakum attack, Mindy wondered if Jonathan would rewind time for her like Superman did for Lois Lane.

Mindy's fingertips brushed a basket. She pulled it out. No wild creature or thorny plant inside, just a mass of jumbled lengths of rope. This was oakum?

Sighing, Bridget said, "Hand me a length."

Mindy handed the basket to Bridget, and she took a white, sodden-looking piece.

Sarah took a hard, black piece covered in what looked like tar or oil.

Mindy took a piece herself, but she hadn't the faintest clue what to do with it.

Sarah and Bridget picked at the rope, untwisting it into cork-screw strands of fiber, each about two feet long.

"I'm a bit embarrassed to admit this," Mindy said, "but I've never picked oakum before. What do I do?"

Sarah showed her how to separate the rope segments like they had. "Then you slide the strand back and forth on your knee with the palm of your hand until all the meshes are loosened."

Mindy did as she was shown. Her hands chafed against the hemp rope as the tar and goop covered her.

Sarah continued. "Then you take this hook between your knees and saw at it to remove the tar and grate the fibers apart—"

"Or you turn smart like me and pick pieces that don't have all the tar," Bridget said with a grin.

"Then you roll the fluffy, clean pieces back together into a loose rope," Sarah finished.

When Mindy finished her strand, brown dust from the rope covered her arms, and her fingers were covered with small cuts and rope burns.

"You do this a lot?" Mindy asked.

Sarah nodded. "Mostly we spin or sew, but we all pick oakum in our spare time," Sarah said. "In a port city like Philadelphia, there is great need. The shipbuilders use the oakum to caulk their ships."

"Widow Madison *says* she shares the proceeds when she sells a batch to the shipbuilders but—"

Sarah frowned. "Be fair, Bridget. Widow Madison shares with us what's left over after she is compensated for our room and board."

"Says you. But I don't think that we cost nearly what she brings in with our work."

As the girls continued to banter, Mindy listened closely for any signs of alien possession. Andros's slick, oozing grin was always a clear indicator, but that was when he wanted to flaunt his possession. Mindy was looking for indications that a disoriented teenager *and* an alien were waking up inside their human host.

During their Civil War adventure, when her friend Chad had finally awoken in his host body, he'd used twenty-first-century slang. Even before he woke up fully, parts of his personality, like his staunch vegetarianism, popped through from time to time.

Mindy wondered what Serena-specific personality traits might pop up. Serena's friends knew her as a flirty social butterfly, but Mindy knew better. If Serena's dominant personality trait popped out of the host body, she'd see a belligerent, annoying girl who would fight with Mindy about anything—the stupider the better.

Their last fight had been about Mindy's orange-and-white teddy bear hamster, Chewie. Full of mischief, as hamsters are, and blind as a bat, as hamsters also tend to be, Chewie had gotten out of his cage and somehow managed to wind up in the bathtub just before Serena went to take a shower.

The bloodcurdling scream had awakened Mindy. Groggy with sleep, she had not exactly been apologetic to Serena, and when Serena had called Chewie an aqua-rat, it was all over. They didn't speak to each other for the rest of the morning.

Before the two could make up properly, Andros had chrono-bombed Serena into the past. Now Mindy would never forgive herself if anything happened to her sister.

Now she might actually be close to finding her sister—as long as she could focus on the task at hand. All she had to do was hang out with the boardinghouse residents and see if any of them showed Serena-like behavior.

Of the two of them, Bridget reminded Mindy more of her sister than Sarah did. It wasn't just that Sarah was pregnant, either. Sarah was too soft-spoken, too, well, *nice* to be Mindy's sister.

Bridget, on the other hand, had Serena's boundless energy—and her need to be in everyone else's business. Bridget looked like she'd rather be in breeches than a skirt any day, and that was Serena too.

Of course the typical mannerisms of a person didn't matter at all. What Mindy was looking for was odd behavior, something atypical for either of them. So far, nothing.

A male whisper filtered through the door. "Hey, Bridget, you in there?"

Bridget tossed her oakum back in the basket and bounced to the door. "Where else would I be, Peyton Lynch?" she whispered, opening the door slowly to prevent the creak that had accompanied Mindy's late entrance earlier.

Peyton tiptoed in exaggeratedly and plopped on the bed behind Sarah and Bridget. "So you're the new girl who's responsible for me getting kicked out of my room," he said.

"I'm sorry. I didn't mean—" Mindy stuttered.

"Oh, I'm just kidding. Not so happy about the men in my bedroom, but I'm definitely elated at adding a third lovely lady to our home."

Sarah rolled her eyes, but Bridget stiffened. Evidently the sharp, dark-haired tomboy didn't appreciate the competition.

"Thanks, I guess," Mindy said, blushing. He *was* quite handsome. And he kind of reminded her of Jonathan—same chin, same broad chest and big muscles.

"In fact, I think we should celebrate our new friends," Peyton said, removing a flask from his coat and taking a swig. He held the flask out toward the girls.

Bridget's eyes lit up, but Sarah sniffed and resumed picking oakum. "You may have time to get all lushy, but the rest of us have work to do. It is our duty to Widow Madison."

"Come on, live a little," Peyton said.

The handsome slacker's language seemed less formal than the girls', almost contemporary at times. And his forward demeanor, although kind of charming to Mindy, seemed odd to Sarah and Bridget. Could she have been so lucky to find Serena on the first day? And was Serena really in a *guy?*

"You should relax sometime," Peyton continued, moving to rub Sarah's shoulders.

Sarah blushed and pulled away. "My husband wouldn't approve. And I have work to do."

The overly familiar gesture made Mindy as uncomfortable as it did Sarah but for a different reason. Mindy hoped Peyton was naturally lecherous, for, if he wasn't, his behavior matched Andros's.

"Come on . . . " Peyton prompted, batting his thick eyelashes at Sarah.

Sarah scooped up her rope and moved to the other bed.

Bridget snorted. "If you *had* a husband, you certainly wouldn't be here."

"He's out to sea, trying to earn money for the child."

"What ship?" Bridget pried.

"It's the *Dominick Terry,* if you must know."

"And in whose employ does he sail on the *Dominick Terry?*"

Sarah swallowed hard. "Captain, uh, Goolsberry, I think."

Bridget arched an eyebrow. "Really? Should we go ask Samuel? He worked down at the docks until he lost his job because of the non-importation rules. I'm sure *he'll* know the name of the captain of the *Dominick Terry.*"

"I told you I wasn't sure."

"You're a liar. There probably isn't even a ship called the *Dominick Terry.* You just don't want to admit that he knocked you up and left you with a bellyful of squeaker."

Sarah's eyes glistened. "I do *too* have a husband."

Mindy felt horrible. It was pretty clear Bridget was giving Sarah grief because Peyton had lavished attention on Sarah.

Peyton bounced playfully onto the bed next to Sarah. "Of course you do, Sarah. But your husband's not here right now, is he? How about a little drink?" He wiggled the flask in front of her.

Sarah's shoulder sagged. "Maybe just one little drink," she said, smiling shyly. "As long as I don't drink enough to get drunk . . . "

"Me too!" Bridget said, joining Sarah and Peyton on the bed.

"You shouldn't," Mindy said. "Sarah's preg—I mean, with child."

"What does that have to do with anything?" Bridget asked. "As long as we don't get too sloshed to work, Widow Madison won't mind."

Mindy contemplated how she'd ever be able to explain the concept of alcohol consumption leading to fetal alcohol syndrome and low birth weight in infants. Instead, she opted for a joke. "But who wants to have a drunk baby inside of them? It seems like it wouldn't take a lot to get a baby plastered. I mean, what if it has to vomit?"

Peyton guffawed, nearly doubling over.

"Ew," Sarah said. "I think I'll pass."

"Killjoy!" Bridget took a gulp. "Hey, this isn't rum! It's wine! Where'd you get wine?"

"From Thomas's stash," Peyton said, grinning.

"You mean he *did* have enumerated goods?" Sarah asked.

"Of course," Peyton said. "He's been selling British goods out of his woodshed for months. When the patriots came, he signaled me to move what I could. I appropriated the wine as my payment."

A meaty fist pounded on the door. "Mindy Gold, I need to see you immediately."

"Under the bed," Bridget hissed at Peyton. Evidently she'd had a bit of experience hiding men in her room.

Peyton slid effortlessly beneath the lumpy bed—clearly having had experience being hidden in women's bedrooms.

"Come in," Sarah said.

As the doorknob turned, Mindy noticed that Bridget still held Peyton's flask. She gestured at it, and Bridget buried the alcohol in the oakum basket, just as Widow Madison entered. She looked like she'd been crying.

The portly Quaker sniffed and straightened, hardening when she saw Mindy.

"Downstairs, Mindy. You and Jonathan have a visitor." The woman's compassionate tone had been replaced with one of frustration and disdain.

"Who is it?" Mindy asked. "We don't know anyone in Philadelphia." Behind the stern Quaker, Jonathan looked equally confused.

"Downstairs," Widow Madison repeated, "and bring your things. You won't be returning."

His Royal Weirdness:

6 Traits That Made King George III "Different"

For some reason, madness and monarchy seem to go hand in hand. There's Juana "The Mad" of Castille, Ludwig II "The Mad" of Bavaria, and Charles VI "The Mad" of France. It appears "Mad" King George III of Great Britain, known for his peculiar habits, was in good company.

Trait #1: He talked to trees

Throughout his adult life, George suffered strange bouts of unexplained illness, including stomach pains, joint aches, and skin problems. As he aged, however, the symptoms became more frequent and far more severe. After 1800, the normally mild-mannered king began to lose it altogether. In one famous episode, he insisted that an oak tree was the king of Prussia and carried on a lengthy imaginary conversation with it. He also saw angels, made lewd comments to women (which was completely out of character for him—see Trait #3), and talked incessantly. At times, doctors were compelled to tie him to a chair or bed to keep him from hurting himself. The cause of all this strange behavior? In the twentieth century, scientists realized that George, like several of his royal relatives, suffered from a genetic disease called porphyria, which can lead to mental breakdown. His well-meaning doctors gave him a medicine containing arsenic, which probably triggered George's episodes and made them more severe.

Trait #2: . . . and he talked funny

Early in life, George developed the habit of ending sentences with the exclamations "What, what?" and "Hey, hey!" For example: "Splendid weather today, what, what?" When his majesty was particularly animated, he would add extra *what*s and *hey*s—sometimes as many as four or five to end an observation or question. The only time he didn't do this was when a bout of porphyria came upon him. In fact, his family and his doctors both learned that the lack of *hey*s and whats meant that the king was going mad again. When the *hey*s and *what*s returned, it meant he was regaining his senses and would soon be perfectly lucid—for a while, anyway.

Trait #3: He was painfully shy with the ladies

Who says kings can get anything they want? You'd think a man in his position would have king-sized confidence, but George was famously shy when it came to members of the opposite sex. In fact, he felt so awkward around them he left it up to his chief advisor, John Stuart, to do his courting for him, claiming that letting Stuart play matchmaker would "save a great deal of trouble." At one point, George took a shine to fifteen-year-old Lady Sarah Lennox, but she didn't pass muster with Stuart, probably because she came from a prominent family, and Stuart feared if she were to gain power, her family might nudge him out of his position as the king's go-to guy. In her place, he delivered seventeen-year-old Charlotte of Mecklenburg-Strelitz, a German princess who wasn't considered a looker. Legend has it that George winced when he first saw Charlotte, but he married her anyway. The union turned out to be a long and fruitful one, lasting fifty-seven years and producing fifteen children!

Trait #4: He was as dull as dishwater

Other kings threw lavish balls, hunted, and built elaborate palaces. George and his wife ate a simple supper of mutton (sheep meat) and Brussels sprouts each evening and went to bed early. If duty called, the king would entertain or attend an evening reception, but he hated to stay up late, much preferring to spend quiet evenings reading books from his splendid library or looking over the voluminous official papers that he insisted on inspecting personally. Worried about putting on weight, the king avoided rich foods and took little wine, and the little wine he did serve at court was reputedly awful. Critics, including the king's children, called the court of George III the dullest in Europe.

Trait #5: He had unusual ideas about parenthood

It's one thing to be a concerned parent. It's another thing to force your royal offspring to stay home and read, sew, and pray all the time. George and Charlotte sheltered their six precious princesses to the point that only two ever married—one in her late twenties and another when she was forty. The youngest, Amelia, may also have married, but if she did, it was in secret and never publicly acknowledged. George and Charlotte did not take the steps required to make matches for their girls and refused to approve relationships that the princesses themselves initiated. The daughters coped in differing ways. Charlotte, the eldest, often quarreled with her mother. Augusta looked after her siblings and, with her sister Mary, seemed to relish a sheltered domestic life. Elizabeth, an amateur artist, busied herself with her paintings. Sophia and Amelia, the youngest, had emotional outbursts and, like their father, suffered bouts of illness. George and Charlotte's parenting strategy didn't quite work: At least one of the unmarried princesses, Sophia, is thought to have given birth to a child out of wedlock.

Trait #6: He had a peculiar obsession with farming

George liked the hands-on experience of working in the fields or garden. He also enjoyed discussing theories about crop breeding, planting strategy, and pest control. When not tending his crops of oats, barley, turnips, and buckwheat or looking after his sheep and other livestock on the royal estate at Kew (now Kew Gardens in Richmond-upon-Thames, an outer borough of London), George indulged his common touch by riding or walking through the countryside, visiting rural villages. He wore ordinary clothes and eschewed guards so that he could strike up conversations with people who didn't realize who they were talking to. What did the king and the commoners talk about? Farming—what else?

Chapter Eight

Mindy didn't recognize the tall, fastidiously dressed blond man standing stiffly in the parlor next to a long-haired gray Irish wolf-hound that came to his waist.

He, however, seemed to know her.

"Mindy Gold, you traitorous rattle-pate," he said. "After all I've invested in you, you run off with my neighbor's best apprentice. You and Jonathan will add a month to your contract for every day you've been gone, and you'll work off what it cost for me to track you down too!"

Mindy would have suspected she and Jonathan were being punk'd if she'd been back home in twenty-first-century Salem, but not only didn't 1775 Philadelphia have any hidden video cameras, but she was pretty sure this officious man wasn't Ashton Kutcher in silk stockings and a powdered wig. "What are you talking about?"

"I'm so disappointed," Widow Madison said, "but I did have a feeling that something was amiss." She turned to the stranger. "I would have never offered shelter to runaway indentured servants, had I known, Mr. Dewitt. You must believe me."

"Of course, of course." Dewitt gave a patronizing smirk. Although he wore a suit much like Jasper's, his was of the finest materials—blue silk brocade, gold trim, and ornate brass buttons. He could have stepped out of an oil painting of one of the founding fathers, except that with his rigid posture and military bearing, he somehow managed to make the ensemble look like an SS uniform.

Dewitt reached down to pat the equally intimidating purebred at his side.

It growled at him.

Dewitt quickly withdrew his hand.

"We're not indentured servants, Widow Madison," Mindy said. "We've never met this man before in our lives. I don't know who he is, but he's not our master."

Dewitt shook his head in mock regret, addressing only the boardinghouse owner. "It's sad, really—all these lies and deceptions just because I won't allow them to marry until she's served her contract."

"Marry?" Jonathan squeaked.

"Of course I thought they might try something like this," Dewitt continued, "so I instructed Jasper to gain their confidences and elope with them, should they decide to try to leave my employ. The message Jasper sent said they'd arrived in Philadelphia, but he'd not been specific as to the location. That's where Zuriel came in." He tried to pet the dog again. It snapped at him.

"He's a bit cranky after the long trip from Virginia. I'd never have found them without him, though."

"What did you do with Jasper?" Mindy asked.

"Why nothing, of course. I knew you wouldn't be pleased when you found out he'd betrayed you, so I sent him ahead. You'll see him again when you return home—though I don't imagine he'll want to see you."

Mindy felt she'd been struck as dumb as Mr. Winsley was blind.

Widow Madison put a hand on Mindy's shoulder. "Time to return to your master, girl."

Folding his arms across his chest, Jonathan stepped in between Mindy and Dewitt. "We are not leaving with this man. He is not our master."

Zuriel growled.

Widow Madison shook her head. "Now I don't abide liars, Mr. Hartthorne. You must leave."

Mindy knew that was the one thing they couldn't do. She couldn't believe Jasper would just abandon them like this, and that meant the man was lying—and that made him dangerous.

"Please, Widow Madison! Please don't make us go with him," Mindy said.

"As an indentured servant, you belong to him. It is not my position to interfere."

"But he beats me, every day," Mindy said.

Widow Madison looked as if she softened a bit, but her words indicated otherwise. "If such a fine gentleman finds fault in you and feels you need correction, you must truly be wicked."

"You know that's not the case. Would a wicked person have helped keep your house from burning down?"

"I am thankful for what you did, it is true, but you both are runaway indentured servants—you have admitted it. There is nothing I can do."

"We should have a choice," Mindy said. "Servants aren't slaves."

Dewitt arched an eyebrow. "They are indeed, at least for the term of their contract. You are as much my property as this dog or my three-cornered hat."

Zuriel cocked his head at an odd angle, making it clear he wasn't pleased about being compared to a turned-up scrap of felt.

Mindy ignored them both and focused on the boardinghouse proprietor. "Please, Widow Madison. If you don't let us stay, I'll just run away again, and maybe next time we won't be as lucky to find someone kind like you who will let us work for our keep."

"You're supposed to be working for your keep with me," Dewitt said, "not for some stranger."

Man, this guy had a lot of nerve. He was really playing up the role. Well, so could she.

Mindy lowered her head, her voice just a cracking whisper. "He does things . . . to me. Please don't make me go."

Widow Madison's eyes glazed with tears. "I can't stop him, child. You have to honor your contract and go with him."

Dewitt sighed. "I'm running out of patience. If you don't come with me, I'll send the constable to enforce my rights."

The tall blond stranger's arrogance continued to shock Mindy. And the level of detail in his fabricated story overwhelmed her. He definitely had the upper hand. Only another time traveler could know this much about them and make it all fit so conveniently. Dewitt was either another Time Stream Investigator or Andros. Neither would reveal himself in front of Widow Madison. They'd have to go with him to find out who he really was.

Mindy turned to Dewitt. "You want us to go with you? Fine. Let's go."

Jonathan dropped his arms. "Mindy, no. This man is an imposter."

"If we can't stay here, we have no other choice," Mindy said.

A slick, self-righteous smile crept across Dewitt's face. "Finally."

"I don't think it's wise—" Jonathan started.

"I'm going. You can either come with us or wait for the constable." Mindy knew full well that Minister Hartthorne wouldn't leave her alone with this man.

Dewitt bowed to Widow Madison. "I apologize for any inconvenience my wayward servants may have caused you. Your kind assistance has been noted."

Widow Madison wrung her hands and then fiddled with her apron. "Safe travels," she said, her uncertainty over her decision obvious.

As soon as the boardinghouse door closed behind them, Jonathan leaned over to whisper in Mindy's ear. "What's wrong with you? This is sheer folly. That man must be possessed by Andros."

Dewitt, who had been leading the way with Zuriel at his side, turned to Jonathan. "I assure you there is no one inside of me—Galagian or otherwise."

"That's just what someone who is possessed would say," Jonathan said. "And I should know." Jonathan had experienced possession firsthand when they had traveled to Bull Run.

"Who *are* you?" Mindy asked the stranger.

"I am an Intelligence Officer of the Free Fascist State. I also happen to be Jasper Gordon's superior officer."

"So if you're one of the good guys, why all the theatrics?"

"Sustaining the flow of the time stream is of paramount importance to the future state." Dewitt looked down his aquiline nose at her. "When an agent has inserted herself into a period in history, she must be extricated in a believable manner so as not to disrupt the flow. The slightest disruption of the time stream can produce a destabilizing effect on the future state that our enemies would be quick to exploit. And we have *many* enemies. You would know all of this if you were a real Time Stream Enforcer," he added.

"I didn't ask for this job," Mindy said. "Jasper said I was needed, that it took a twenty-first-century teen to identify another twenty-first-century teen."

"Jasper!" Dewitt barked out a bitter laugh. "Do not imagine for a moment that anyone at command cares what that little runt thinks."

Mindy bristled. "Why are you guys so mean to him anyway? He does the best he can for you."

Dewitt's eyes narrowed as he regarded her. "For certain things, we cannot do without him, unfortunately. But when officers of the State formulate strategy, we are not in the habit of consulting subhumans."

"*Subhumans?*" Mindy could not believe what she was hearing. "What are you people—the chrono-Gestapo? Where do you get off calling Jasper a subhuman? Are you saying that because he's Irish or something?"

Dewitt laughed—with real amusement this time. "Or something. You really don't know, do you? He's not an Irishman. He's not a man at all. He's a fairy."

"Well, I'm glad to see that homophobia is alive and well in the twenty-sixth century," Mindy said dryly.

"No, dear, not that kind of fairy. I mean the kind they make calendars about at Barnes & Noble." He looked at her, but she still wasn't getting it. "The kind with wings."

Born on the Second of July:

6 Little-Known Facts About the Declaration of Independence

Got an extra nine million bucks lying around? That might be enough to buy one of the original copies of the Declaration of Independence. Before you invest, though, get to know the true history of one of America's most famous documents.

Little-known fact #1: July 4 should really be celebrated on July 2

When you enjoy the fireworks next Independence Day, keep in mind that you're celebrating a few days late. While July 4 is traditionally thought to be the day the United States declared independence from Great Britain, this event actually took place on July 2, when the Second Continental Congress passed the Lee Resolution. Written and introduced by delegate Richard Henry Lee of Virginia, it began, "Resolved, That these United Colonies are, and of right ought to be, free and independent States." Two days later, on July 4, the congress voted to approve the Declaration, which was a more formal statement of the reasons for independence. The Declaration bore July 4 as its date, and that's the date everyone remembers.

Little-known fact #2: The original draft was about twice as long

Even great writers like Thomas Jefferson need editors. The original draft of the Declaration that Jefferson submitted to the Second Continental Congress was about twice as long as the final version. What got left on the cutting-room floor? Jefferson later noted that passages that were too critical of the English were "struck out, lest they should give them offense." Also among the deleted material was a stern condemnation of the slave trade, which Jefferson included even though he himself was conflicted about the issue of slavery and was a slave-owner. Southern delegates to the congress made sure the bit about slavery was left out.

Little-known fact #3: Some famous phrases were "borrowed" from other documents

Guess they didn't have footnotes back in colonial days. Jefferson may have been a brilliant writer, but some of his most memorable turns of phrase were borrowed from elsewhere. The Declaration was based in part on an earlier document called the Virginia Declaration of Rights, written by George Mason, also one of the signatories of the Declaration. Jefferson's most famous phrase, "life, liberty, and the pursuit of happiness," closely echoes a phrase of English philosopher John Locke's, who wrote about a right to "life, liberty, and estate." The precise meaning of the three words Jefferson added, "pursuit of happiness," has been the subject of 230 years of debate. Some think he defined "happiness" as material well-being, while others suggest he literally meant "property."

Little-known fact #4: There's more writing on the reverse side

A few years ago, a movie called *National Treasure* suggested that if you flipped over the Declaration, you'd find directions to a hidden treasure written in a secret code. Unfortunately, real life is more mundane than Hollywood's version. What's really on the reverse side of the Declaration is a label written by some long-ago federal file clerk. It reads: "Original Declaration of Independence dated 4th July 1776."

Little-known fact #5: It ain't aging gracefully

The Declaration is more than 230 years old—and it looks it. Not only is the document badly stained, it's so faded that many of the famous signatures are barely visible. Since 1951, preservation scientists at the National Archives have treated the Declaration with the utmost care, employing state-of-the-art techniques to prevent further deterioration. If you visit the Declaration on your next trip to Washington, D.C., you'll find it housed in a special case filled with an inert gas.

Little-known fact #6: The first printing was a limited edition

You'd think the founding fathers would have printed thousands of copies of their Declaration. Actually, the congress originally printed just two hundred copies—not enough to circulate in Philadelphia, let alone the thirteen colonies. Why such a small print run? The Dunlap Broadside, as the printing was called after printer John Dunlap, was intended to be read aloud in public gathering places, not distributed to individual readers. Today, there are only twenty-five copies of the Dunlap Broadside in existence, and the last one to change hands sold for $8.14 million.

Chapter Nine

"Wait a minute—he's a *what?!*" Mindy spluttered. Beside her, Jonathan looked like he was having a hard time keeping up as well.

Dewitt raised an eyebrow archly, looking amused. "Fairies are an indispensable tool of the State. Not all of the State's tools are very appealing, but there you are."

"Wait—excuse me a minute," Mindy persisted, "But I want to get this straight. Why would *fairies* be working for the Free Fascist State of the future? Can you really produce a coherent explanation of this, or are you just trying to give me a seizure so you can teleport me home?"

Dewitt shrugged. "Given all you know already about the future, I see no harm in your knowing this—particularly if it convinces you to make a bit less of a fuss about going home. Fairies, you see, have a natural affinity for time travel, teleportation, manipulation of the time stream, and things of that nature. The State owes its stability in large part to its success in harnessing these capacities that the fairies naturally enjoy and putting them to good use. What's more, most human agents, even those with high tempose levels, cannot withstand extended time-travel as well as the fairies, so they're indispensable for going back centuries into the past. It's true that they're mischievous and uncooperative by nature, but don't worry—they're quite safe. Free State technology allows us to keep them on a *very* tight leash."

"What—you mean you've enslaved them?" Mindy flushed.

"Call it what you will."

"What have you done with Jasper—I want to talk with him."

"He's . . . where we can keep an eye on him. He's getting a chance to consider the error of his ways before we let him complete his assignment."

"But he's helping me find my sister. She's in this time period and probably has smallpox."

"Well, that *is* a shame. But the least disruptive thing for the time stream is to let nature take its course." He hastened to add before Mindy could interrupt him: "We *do* care about your sister—all actual humans are of great value to the State. But the State has to come first. She is not more important than the integrity and stability of all of human history. She just isn't."

Mindy pushed down her fury and made her voice as cool as possible. "May I *please* speak to Jasper?"

Dewitt laughed. "You still don't get it, do you? Jasper does not care *at all* about your sister. In this matter, his interests and the State's are perfectly aligned. The person he cares about finding, and the person *we* urgently want found, is Jasper's brother."

Mindy blinked.

"Jasper has a brother?" Jonathan asked.

"Why, of course. You know him intimately, I believe. His brother is Andros." Dewitt took obvious pleasure in witnessing their consternation. "*Now* do you still think Jasper is going to help you?"

Mindy turned away, unable to speak. Andros was Jasper's *brother*? The alien who had put her sister's life in danger was the brother of her time-cop guide? And they both were fairies?

Apart from the sheer shock of the situation, Mindy couldn't begin to express how angry she was at that very moment—at Jasper, at this mean-spirited little chrono-fascist, at the futility of the whole situation.

"What about my sister?" Mindy said through gritted teeth. "You're really planning to let her die an agonizing death of smallpox in her host body, and then let her spirit be banished to the Void, when you could just find her in the boarding house and transport her home?"

"It's unfortunate, I admit, but unavoidable. We cannot risk disrupting the time stream any further."

"Let us stay and find her," Jonathan said. "We have a week, maybe two before anyone in the house displays symptoms. There is still time to locate Mindy's sister."

"No, no, no," Dewitt said. "Out of the question. I can't risk untrained civilians doing additional damage to the time stream."

"I won't go. Not without my sister."

"You have no choice in the matter." Dewitt took a chronolyzer from his pocket and started the calculations required for time-travel.

Jonathan straightened his shoulders. "I won't allow it. We are not going to abandon Mindy's sister." He lunged at the officer and knocked Dewitt's chronolyzer out of his hand and into the rainwater barrel he had been standing next to.

Jonathan grabbed Mindy's hand and pulled her down the cobblestone street.

"I can't believe you just did that!" Mindy said.

"We are not leaving your sister behind."

Mindy glanced over her shoulder. Dewitt plunged his arm into the barrel in search of the chronolyzer as Zuriel watched intently.

"Why isn't he sending the dog after us?" Mindy said. "We'd never be able to outrun him. Irish wolfhounds were bred to run down wolves." *And kill them,* Mindy thought.

A two-wheeled, two-passenger chaise with a dainty white mare harnessed to it loomed up ahead.

"We'll take the carriage," Jonathan said.

"Wait," Mindy said as Jonathan prepared to climb aboard. "The streets are too narrow. We need to be maneuverable. Unhitch the horse."

As Jonathan quickly freed the white mare, Mindy looked back at Dewitt. His fine blue silk brocade suit was drenched. He muttered something to Zuriel. The dog barked, and Dewitt took a step backward.

The gray Irish wolfhound began to shrink, its thick, wiry coat becoming slick short hair; his face growing more pear-shaped; his front paws morphing into flippers; and his back paws fusing together to form a tail.

Zuriel barked again, but this time as a gray seal. He dove into the barrel and came back up with the chronolyzer in his mouth.

Mindy mounted the white horse Jonathan had unhitched, offering her hand to help him up. "This time I'm going to drive," she said.

Jonathan slid his arms around her waist. "Are you sure?"

Mindy goaded the horse, and they took off down the street at a gallop. As they turned the corner, Mindy risked another glance back. Instead of fuming in the street like some cartoon villain, Dewitt was struggling to stay atop an imposing dapple-gray stallion. The tall intelligence officer dug his heels hard into Zuriel's sides, weaving his fingers through the horse's mane and yanking on it in an attempt to stay seated. Zuriel did not seem pleased.

Mindy and Jonathan's mare, however, seemed happy to be free of the heavy carriage and sprinted forward as if she had been set to gambol in a field of wildflowers. She obeyed Mindy's firm yet gentle commands without pause, taking one sharp turn after another.

They could hear Zuriel's hooves clattering on the cobblestones but always kept several turns ahead of him.

"If they can't see us to follow us," Jonathan said, "how are they keeping up?"

"It's the horseshoes. If we can hear them, they can hear us." Suddenly Mindy had an idea. "Hold on tight," she said.

Mindy pushed the mare even harder, took a rapid succession of sharp turns, and then guided the horse down a narrow side alley to wait.

They held their breath as the thunder of Zuriel's hooves grew louder and louder with each passing second.

The mare shifted, whinnying softly.

Mindy stroked the mare's shoulder to calm her. "Hold on, girl," she whispered.

Jonathan reached up to take Mindy's other hand, squeezing it.

The cacophonous clatter of Zuriel's hooves slowly began to fade, and after what seemed like an eternity, it disappeared all together.

"You're amazing," Jonathan said.

Mindy blushed as she backed the horse out of the alley and headed them in the opposite direction. "We need to make sure they don't double back or anything. We need plenty of distance between us and them."

"Where did you learn to ride like that?" Jonathan asked.

"My dad used to take me," she said. "I haven't ridden in a couple years, though. Good animals never let you down." She leaned forward and patted the mare's neck. "Thank you," she whispered.

The horse whickered appreciatively.

After a few more minutes without any sign of pursuit, Mindy pulled the horse to a stop outside a tavern on the corner of Second Street and Walnut.

"We need a plan," Mindy said. As she dismounted, her skirt rode up around her waist and the chronolyzer clattered to the street.

"It's a blessing it didn't fall out during our escape," Jonathan said, joining her on the ground.

"Chronolyzer, what's up with Dewitt's dog-slash-seal-slash-horse?" she asked.

I CANNOT REFUSE TO ANSWER YOUR QUERIES AND WILL OTHERWISE PERFORM THE FUNCTIONS FOR WHICH I WAS PROGRAMMED, the chronolyzer displayed. BUT MAY I FIRST SUGGEST THAT YOU TURN YOURSELVES IN TO DEWITT AT ONCE? YOUR CHANCES OF EVADING AN INTELLIGENCE OFFICER AND A CYBER-BLOODHOUND ARE MICROSCOPICALLY SMALL.

"Just answer my question," Mindy snapped. "We've heard about enough of your opinions."

NO NEED TO BE TESTY. NO DOUBT I'LL SOON BE IN THE POSSESSION OF SOMEONE MORE PRUDENT THAN YOURSELVES. THE CYBER-BLOODHOUND IS A PROTOTYPE OF THE RESEARCH DIVISION OF THE TIME STREAM INVESTIGATIONS UNIT. IT HAS A METALLIC ENDOSKELETON THAT ALLOWS IT TO TRANSFORM INTO ANY PERIOD-APPROPRIATE ANIMAL.

"So it's a robot?"

CYBORG, ACTUALLY. IT'S PART ANIMAL, PART ROBOT. JUST LIKE YOU WEAR A CLOTHING RECEIVER TO GIVE YOU PERIOD CLOTHING, ITS COLLAR CONTAINS A BIO-RECEIVER. ITS MASTER CAN DIAL UP ANY APPROPRIATE BIO-SKIN FOR THE ANIMAL—FEATHERS, FUR, OR EVEN SCALES.

"Maybe we should get out of the street," Jonathan said.

SOUND LOGIC, PREACHER MAN, the chronolyzer typed. THE CYBER-BLOODHOUND WAS MADE TO HUNT ALIEN BEASTIES FAR MORE CRAFTY AND RESOURCEFUL THAN THE TWO OF YOU. INSIDE IS DEFINITELY GOOD BECAUSE, BY MY CALCULATIONS, IF YOU STAY OUTSIDE, THERE IS A 98.3 PERCENT LIKELIHOOD THAT THE CYBER-BLOODHOUND WILL FIND YOU WITHIN TEN MINUTES.

Your Name in Sites:

5 Founding Fathers and the Stuff Named for Them

You can't go anywhere in America without running into a *Washington* this or a *Jefferson* that. And the founding fathers' names aren't confined to the States, either.

Eponym #1: Washington pie

Washington is, hands-down, the winner of the prize for "most things named after him." In addition to the nation's capital and an entire western state, his name has been slapped on thirty-three U.S. counties, innumerable schools, four mountains, an island in Kiribati (an island nation in the Pacific), and streets in places ranging from Hamburg, Germany, to Santo Domingo, Dominican Republic. Washington is also the only president, to the best of our knowledge, to have a type of cake named after him. Called *Washington pie* (even though it's actually a cake), this gooey dessert was probably named for Washington because of its cherry filling.

Eponym #2: Madison Square Garden

You might not think there's a natural connection between the New York Knicks and our fourth president. But it's right there in lights: Madison

Square Garden, the entertainment complex named, albeit indirectly, for one of our founding fathers, James Madison. Although it's located at Penn Station today, the original Garden building was located on Madison Avenue (naturally) just a few blocks up the street from New York's Madison Square. Interestingly, out of all of the presidents, Madison—a native Virginian—probably gets the most signage in the Big Apple.

Eponym #3: Jeffersonian architecture

If you want to impress architecture buffs, you might try saying "Ah, you'd call that building Jeffersonian, wouldn't you?" while stroking your chin thoughtfully. Although he never trained as an architect, Jefferson mastered the discipline, as demonstrated by his famous designs for the University of Virginia and his home, Monticello. His designs reflected his belief that a building should please the senses and engage the mind as well as provide practical shelter. If you see an American building with round rooms, columns, arched windows, and a domed roof, chances are its architect found inspiration in Jefferson and his buildings.

Eponym #4: Monrovia, Capital of Liberia, Africa

What's a founding father's name doing all the way over in Africa? James

Monroe is the only U.S. president with the honor of having a foreign capital named for him—Monrovia, Liberia. Established in the early 1820s by Jehudi Ashmun, a white American, the West African colony of Liberia provided an African homeland for freed slaves and freeborn blacks who wished to leave the United States. The capital city was named after Monroe, the then-current U.S. president, to honor the colony's American roots.

Eponym #5: Lafayette, Capital of Cajun Cooking

Okay, so he wasn't technically a founding father. But there are at least sixty-two cities, towns, and counties in the United States named Fayetteville, La Fayette, Lafayette, or Fayette—including Fayetteville, Arkansas, home of the University of Arkansas, and Lafayette, Louisiana, home of Cajun cooking. All are named for the Frenchman Marquis de La Fayette. So how did a French guy get so many American places named after him? Not only did La Fayette command American troops as a general in Washington's army, playing a decisive role in forcing the British surrender at Yorktown, but he also helped persuade French King Louis XVI to join the war on the American side. Without French troops, ships, and supplies, the Americans probably wouldn't have won the Revolutionary War.

Chapter Ten

Mindy sighed. She didn't need any more bad news. "You know, if I ever got a chance to program you, I'd make it so you could only present your statistics in a positive manner."

THERE IS A 1.7 PERCENT CHANCE THAT THE CYBORG DOG WITH STATE-OF-THE-ART TRACKING CAPABILITIES WILL NOT FIND YOU.

"Oh, that's much better," Jonathan said.

BUT IF IT DOES FIND YOU, the chronolyzer continued, IT'S NOT EXACTLY PROGRAMMED TO FETCH YOU YOUR DOC MARTENS AND THE LATEST ISSUE OF TIME STREAM INVESTIGATOR FORTNIGHTLY.

"That's okay," Mindy said. "I let my subscription lapse anyhow."

Inside the tavern, they sat at one of several clusters of elegant tables and chairs, stalling when the prickly, well-endowed barmaid demanded their order. No money meant no food or drink. Mindy's stomach growled in protest.

The tavern was more like a premier restaurant than a dive bar—not at all what Mindy had expected. The main room was spacious and airy, containing refined furniture and expensive trappings. Doorways promised other less public rooms, and stairs led to rooms for hire.

"I wish we could order something," Mindy said the second time they had to turn away the persistent barmaid. "I'm so hungry I'd eat the leather off the sole of my shoe if I weren't a vegetarian."

"Whatever plan we make, it should include food," Jonathan agreed.

Every muscle in Mindy's body ached from prolonged tensing, and her head still pounded to the cadence of Zuriel's hooves. She wanted to curl up someplace safe and warm and sleep for about 700 years. "Do you think Jasper is really Andros's brother?" she asked softly. It grieved her to even ask the question.

"It would appear so. I don't see why Dewitt would make that up."

"I can't believe he's just been lying to us all this time, after all we've been through together."

Jonathan reached across the table and took Mindy's hand. His hand was warm and rough. "You must not dwell on the past. You must be strong for Serena."

Mindy choked back tears. "But what can I do for her now? We've escaped Dewitt and Zuriel for the time being, but between the smallpox and the lies Dewitt told Widow Madison about us, I can't even get near the house, much less interview the residents to determine who might be harboring Serena.

"And forget about dosing everyone with tempose. Assuming everyone ate the tempose-laden soup I made, nobody has enough of the chemical inside of them to allow us to transport Serena back to her own time, even if we could find the host. There's nothing we can do."

The tenacious barmaid, who had been serving the two gentlemen at the table next to them, turned around. "You can order food—that's what you can do," she said, talking animatedly with her hands. "If you're not eating or drinking you're leaving."

"Uh . . . " Not only was Mindy still starving, but the chronolyzer's 1.7 percent probability of them evading Zuriel for good would become a zero-percent chance if they went back outside without a plan.

A spirited elderly man with thinning, shoulder-length gray hair got up from the neighboring table. Tall yet stout, he wore a plain, knee-length brown velvet coat and leaned on a cane. Even without the round, sliver-rimmed spectacles, Mindy would have recognized him immediately.

"They'll be joining us, Penny dear," Benjamin Franklin said.

Mindy swallowed hard as the oldest revolutionary gazed at her, his gray eyes steady with a hint of mirth. "I couldn't help overhearing your fascinating conversation. I am transfixed by your fanciful speech. Is it an experiment or perhaps some kind of game?"

"We're not from around here," Mindy stammered.

"That, I did notice," Franklin said, smiling. "Enchanting lady, would you and your companion do me the honor of joining us for our meal, so I may hear more of your exotic speech—and you?"

Mindy's growling stomach didn't allow her the courtesy of a consultation with the Rev before she responded. "Oh, that would be super. Thank you."

Franklin held out his hand, and Mindy took it awkwardly, following his lead as he guided her to his table. He gave his dinner partner, a genial man in his late thirties, a telling look, and the younger man vacated his chair for Mindy. Jonathan wedged uncomfortably into the narrow seat next to her.

Although Franklin looked old enough to be Mindy's grandfather, he had a frank and open demeanor and an agelessness that charmed her.

"I fear I've been a horrible cad," he said, "but when you near seven decades, propriety and politeness simply do not matter as much as enjoying the life you've made for yourself and others. Will you forgive me, dear lady?"

Mindy sighed. She could listen to his lyrical turns of phrase all night. "But what have you done to require forgiveness?" she asked.

"I've completely failed to introduce my companion and myself." He gestured at the young man on the other side of Jonathan. "This is my friend Edward Biddle, and my name is Dr. Benjamin Franklin." He leaned in conspiratorially. "But you, my enticing flower, may call me Ben."

Jonathan cleared his throat. Mindy imagined Franklin's overly familiar tone and demeanor would seem scandalous to a Puritan minister. Too bad for Hartthorne. How many times did you get to have dinner with one of the founding fathers?

Mindy leaned back in her chair. "I'm Mindy, Mindy Gold. And this is my friend Jonathan Hartthorne."

"*Minister* Jonathan Hartthorne," he amended, his emerald eyes clouding over.

Mindy cocked her head at him but didn't say anything. Jonathan hadn't introduced himself as a minister since they'd left Salem and started time-traveling together. Maybe he needed his title as a crutch or a protection—but from what? From a charming old man like Franklin?

"I am so very pleased to make your acquaintance, Minister Hartthorne."

"Unfortunately we cannot stay," Jonathan said.

"Long," Mindy added. "We cannot stay *long*." She glared at Jonathan. Here they had the world-famous writer, diplomat, scientist, and inventor offering to buy them dinner when they had empty bellies and even emptier pockets, and he wanted to go?

Mindy had been fascinated by Ben Franklin since her fifth-grade teacher Mrs. Wagner showed the *Ben and Me* cartoon in class. Every cool thing she'd learned about colonial America somehow seemed to involve Franklin in one way or another—from publishing *Poor Richard's Almanac* to brokering peace between England and France at the end of the American Revolution. She adored him even more when she discovered that like her, he had become a vegetarian in his teens.

Of course it was one thing to see a two-dimensional representation of the famous founding father chatting with a precocious cartoon mouse and another to see a living, breathing version of the real man sitting before you drinking a pint of ale. She wasn't ready to give that up.

"We cannot stay *at all*," Jonathan said, standing. "We have a task to complete, or are you forgetting why we are here?" He steepled his fingers. "Come, Mindy."

"Women are not dogs," Franklin said. "Treat them as such and you must watch out for their bite." He smiled slyly.

"My business is not yours, sir," Jonathan said.

Mindy's voice lowered. "And *my* business is none of yours, *Minister*. I'm not ready to leave. If you want to go, then go."

"Very well," Jonathan said. "I take my leave of you, Dr. Franklin." He stalked toward the door.

"I don't know what's wrong with him," Mindy said. "Maybe I should go after him."

"I would regret losing your company," Franklin said. "I so wanted to hear about this substance called *tempose* and your travels through time—especially from one so enchanting."

Oh, great. Like she hadn't already mucked up the time stream enough. Now she'd baited one of history's great geniuses with the idea of time-travel—700 or so years ahead of schedule. She had to stay, at least long enough to do damage control.

Frowning and agitatedly talking with her hands again, the buxom barmaid, Penny, stopped Jonathan at the door. Mindy couldn't hear what Jonathan said to Penny, and when he gestured over his shoulder at Mindy and then turned back, the barmaid giggled. Jonathan smiled at the well-endowed girl, but Mindy saw his gaze dart back to the table.

She didn't know for sure if Jonathan was flirting with the barmaid. The barmaid could have been doing all the flirting, but it *looked* suspicious from where Mindy was sitting.

Mindy leaned in close to Dr. Franklin. "It's like you guessed," she said. "They're all just fanciful stories Jonathan and I tell each other for entertainment—nothing more."

Penny had taken another step or two closer to Jonathan and now rested her hand on his thick biceps. He shifted uncomfortably, but even so, the couple could have been posing for the cover of a torrid romance novel.

"Then entertain *me,* my bewitching beauty. Tell me the tale you shared with Minister Hartthorne." He cradled her hand, his thin, wrinkled skin smooth and cool to the touch.

"I really should go after Jonathan," Mindy said.

Franklin pouted good-naturedly. "If you must, my dear. Perhaps I will see you tomorrow morning at the procession?"

"I'm afraid not."

Undaunted, Franklin continued. "Edward and I are delegates to the Second Continental Congress, and I understand they expect us all to strut through the streets in our carriages and finery before we convene at the State House. I'm not fond of such peacockery, but it *would* delight me to see you there tomorrow. Perhaps you'll reconsider?"

"Perhaps," Mindy said. "I thank you for your kindness and hospitality, Dr. Franklin." She stood up, hesitating, then bent back down and bestowed a single kiss on his forehead. "If you lived where I do," she whispered, "you'd be a rock star."

She turned toward the door, leaving Franklin staring after her in puzzled bemusement. Both Jonathan and the overly friendly barmaid Penny were gone.

From the chronolyzer´s hard drive . . .

Revolutionary War Superlatives:

Ben Franklin's Yearbook

You know how some people are good at everything? Ben Franklin was one of those people. Back in his day, he was a leading writer, scientist, politician, publisher, inventor, do-gooder, and diplomat. If high school yearbooks had been around back then, he would have swept the superlatives section.

Superlative #1: Most Likely to Succeed

Franklin's early years were remarkably humble. He attended school for two years, and when he was just ten he began working full-time for his father, a candle and soap maker. He taught himself to write in the style of famous English essayists by copying their writings from old issues of periodicals. By age twenty-four, he was master of his own print shop, using skills he had acquired as a writer and printer through an apprenticeship. By age forty-one, he had amassed enough of a fortune that he could afford to retire early. Instead of moving to Florida and taking up golf, however, he continued to thrive as a businessman and journalist, all the while continuing his self-education. He taught himself foreign languages, political philosophy, science, engineering, and music—skills that would all come in handy, to different extents, in his later careers as a scientist and statesman.

Superlative #2: Class Clown

Sure, there were other funny guys in colonial America, but Franklin's humor writing was so popular that many scholars credit him with inventing a brand-new, distinctly *American* style of humor. Writing as his alter ego, Richard Saunders, Franklin published the famous *Poor Richard's Almanac* annually from 1732 to 1757. The almanac featured folksy sayings and proverbs, such as "God helps those who help themselves," promoting the simple virtues of hard work, common sense, thrift, and healthy living. Scholars say Franklin created a tradition of sly American social criticism couched in country values, a tradition that would later encompass such works as Mark Twain's *The Adventures of Huckleberry Finn.*

Superlative #3: Most Likely to Save the World

There are countless stories about Franklin's generosity and good deeds. Realizing that Philadelphia lacked intellectual institutions, he founded a club that would become the prestigious American Philosophical Society and an academy that would eventually become the University of Pennsylvania. Scholars involved with such institutions needed better access to books, which at the time were expensive and scarce, so Franklin founded the nonprofit Library Company of Philadelphia, still an important institution today. On a visit to Boston, Franklin recognized that Bostonians' fire-fighting efforts were better organized than Pennsylvanians'. Franklin campaigned for better fire prevention measures and organized the first volunteer fire company in America.

Superlative #4: Most Creative

Franklin is responsible for a slew of inventions. His creations include a more efficient heating stove, the lightning rod, the odometer (to record the distance traveled by a vehicle), and the armonica, an ingenious musical instrument that produces sounds like those you can make by running a moistened finger along the edge of a crystal goblet. As a middle-aged man, Franklin was bothered by the need to use one pair of spectacles to look into the distance and another to see things close up. Franklin arranged for a lens maker to cut his lenses in half and fit one half of each into a single frame. Thus the bifocal was born.

Superlative #5: Most Likely to Win the Nobel Prize for Physics

We've all heard the famous story about how Franklin discovered electricity by flying a kite in a lightning storm. What he actually did was cause static electricity—the electricity that builds in the atmosphere before a lightning strike—to travel from the atmosphere down the kite string into a Leyden jar, which was an early kind of electrical storage battery. By showing that this atmospheric energy (the same energy that nature releases in concentrated form through lightning bolts) is identical to the static electricity that can be generated by friction, Franklin established that lightning is indeed electricity. Through separate experiments, Franklin developed a theory about the positive and negative charges of electricity that dominated the field of study for many decades. Science historians say that if there had been a Nobel Prize for Physics in the eighteenth century, Franklin would have won it.

Superlative #6: Biggest Nerd

Long before Al Gore taught us about the dangers of global warming, Franklin taught the world a thing or two about the environment. On one of his several voyages to England and back, Franklin began to investigate why sailing to America took so much longer than sailing to England. He realized that in addition to the prevailing winds, a warm ocean current flowing to the northeast was at work. By taking temperature readings and making other observations, Franklin charted the route of this flow, which today is known to originate in the Gulf of Mexico and to moderate the climate of Ireland, Great Britain, and northern Europe.

Chapter Eleven

Mindy stepped out of the tavern and into the warm spring night, expecting to see the Puritan minister and the wanton barmaid lip-locked beneath the streetlight.

Nothing.

The white mare that had served them so spectacularly stood tied where they'd left her. Mindy walked over to the tree and wrapped her arms around the mare's neck. "At least *you* didn't leave me," Mindy said.

The horse whinnied.

A low, melodious voice came from the base of the tree trunk. "And you think I would?"

Mindy peered around the mare. Jonathan sat in the dark with his back against the elm—alone except for a plump gray pigeon roosting on the limb above his head.

"Well, you *did*."

"I thought you wanted some time alone with the *charming* Dr. Franklin."

"Jonathan, he's old enough to be my grandfather."

"More accurately, your great grandfather. Not that it seemed to bother you." He stood up, straightening his blue linen coat.

"I found him to be an interesting older gentleman. That's all."

"And he found you a transfixing, exquisite flower—among other things."

"Why do you even care?"

Jonathan folded his arms across his chest. "The question is, why do *you* care? We have work to do and you're tarrying with a lecherous old man."

Mindy stiffened. "I'm going to cut you some slack because you don't know what a genius that man is, but—"

"Genius? You hardly spent ten minutes with him!"

"He's famous, Jonathan, one of the most important people in American history. One of America's founding fathers—"

"Founding *philanderer,* maybe."

Mindy threw her hands up in the air. "You say you're a man of reason—of logic and intellect. Did you lose your principles down the front of that loose barmaid's corset?"

"And did you lose your morals in the good Dr. Franklin's lap?"

Stunned into silence, Mindy could only stare at him.

Minister Hartthrone blanched. "Mindy, I'm sorry. I really didn't mean—"

"Not another word."

His fingertips brushed her arm. "But—"

She yanked back. "Get away from me." She turned her back on him and marched into the darkened streets of Philadelphia alone.

Around her, narrow brick homes lined brick streets flanked with brick sidewalks. It was as if the city had armor.

What had gotten into Jonathan? It just wasn't like him at all. Was he jealous, like really jealous? To be jealous, you had to like someone. There was no way Jonathan could like her because he had said such mean and horrible things to her.

Jonathan wasn't the only friend who had turned his back on Mindy. She'd thought Jasper was her friend too, but he'd turned out to be lying to her the whole time and was really the brother of the creature who'd put her sister into a coma.

Mindy's stomach sunk. Andros. She'd totally forgotten about him. Jonathan was right. There wasn't any time to waste. They needed to find their way back to Widow Madison's boardinghouse right away. She just hoped that after their fight, Jonathan would still listen to her.

Mindy found Minister Hartthorne sitting on a bench outside the tavern, his elbows on his knees, staring at the ground. The roly-poly gray pigeon from the elm tree was his only companion. The pudgy bird was perched on the back of the bench, eyes closed. As Mindy approached, the pigeon took flight, landing on the upper branch of a nearby oak.

"I'm so sorry," Mindy said, her voice cracking. "I should never have stormed off like that. I—"

Jonathan took both her hands in his. "I am the one who needs to make amends." His deep green eyes radiated sincerity and genuine regret.

Mindy melted. "We've got enough enemies. Let's not add each other to our lists."

Jonathan squeezed her hands and released them. "Agreed." He smiled.

Mindy didn't want to see that smile fade, but she had to tell him. "Andros might be in the boardinghouse."

Jonathan stiffened. "Why didn't you say something before?"

"I wasn't sure at first, and I'm still not. It's hard to figure out what's odd behavior and what's not when you're faced with a house full of strangers."

"Which one is he?"

"Since Andros can body-hop, he could be in anyone now, but we've seen odd behavior from Peyton, Mr. Winsley, Bridget, and even Widow Madison herself." She filled him in on Peyton's sudden lasciviousness and Bridget's intense jealousy, and he'd already seen Mr. Winsley's tantrum after the fire and Widow Madison's meltdown over smallpox.

"Considering the circumstances, though, each of those could be normal responses," Jonathan countered.

"Or it could be Andros, which means we need to get back to the boardinghouse as soon as possible. If he finds his alien friend first and extracts him, Serena will get sent to the Void."

"So we go back to the boardinghouse and find Serena first."

"With Dewitt and Zuriel still looking for us? We'll never get within a mile of the place."

Jonathan rubbed his square jaw thoughtfully. "I'm not sure that is a valid assumption. Dewitt was with us when we left the boarding-house, so he knows we're not there currently."

"But he knows I want to find my sister, and that's where she is. He's stupid if he thinks we won't go back. And of all the things Dewitt is, stupid is not one of them."

"Correct, but the man is also arrogant. He told us he wanted to prevent us from doing additional damage to the time stream. It's likely Dewitt still believes he can track and capture us first, then handle the boardinghouse."

Mindy started to feel hope return, if only just a little bit. "So if we get back there first—"

Mindy peered around Jonathan's shoulder, her words catching in her throat.

"What's wrong?" Jonathan asked, following her blank stare.

"*Flying pig!*" Mindy shouted.

Flash History Review:

10 Terms That Scream "American Revolution"

Proclamations, treaties, and Intolerable Acts—the Revolution was fought not only on the battlefields but also in a war of words.

Term #1: French and Indian War (1754–1763)

The French and Indian War, called the Seven Years' War in its European phase, was the American phase of a struggle between France and Britain to control colonial territory. America focused on the issue of who owned the upper Ohio River Valley—Britain or France. By defeating the French and their Native American allies, Britain gained all of what had been New France east of the Mississippi. It was a vast region stretching from Newfoundland to Lake Superior in what is now Canada and from the Hudson Bay to the Gulf of Mexico. The war was tremendously expensive for the British. The tax measures that led to the American Revolution were Parliament's attempts to get the colonists to help pay for the war.

Term #2: Proclamation of 1763

Colonists saw the end of the French and Indian War as a great opportunity to push westward, acquiring new lands and new income from the natural resources—especially lucrative animal furs—of the interior. With the Proclamation of 1763, a royal order protecting the lands of Native Americans, the British put the breaks of the colonists' dreams of westward expansion. Britain was trying to establish peaceful relations with the tribes, most of whom had sided with the French during the war. American colonists, however, felt great enmity toward Native Americans, especially those who had aided the French. They felt that Native Americans had no land rights whatsoever. By restricting colonists' movement west, the British stirred up intense resentment.

Term #3: Sugar Act (1764)

The Sugar Act was an extension of an earlier, largely unenforced tax on molasses and sugar. It stirred up resentment and rebellious feelings among the colonists, who saw the new tax on wine, beer, coffee, tobacco, and cloth as an impingement on American trade—especially trade with the Dutch. Under an earlier set of laws called the Navigation Acts, all such trade with ships that were neither British nor colonial was technically smuggling. The British government, intent on getting the colonists to help pay for the recent French and Indian war, intended to crack down on illegal trade and tax much more of what the Americans imported.

Term #4: First Currency Act of 1764

Until 1764, each colony printed its own paper money, or colonial scrip. (As a young printer, Benjamin Franklin scored a business coup by snagging the contract to print Pennsylvania's scrip.) The scrip was what is called fiat currency, meaning it had no inherent value but was simply an agreed-upon currency for use within a colony. Britain wanted to suppress the use of such money to discourage off-the-books deals that went untaxed and so passed the Currency Act of 1764, which prohibited the colonies from issuing their own paper money. The colonists saw this as more unjustified meddling in their economy. The Currency Act of 1764 should not be confused with the Currency Act of 1751, which limited—but did not ban—the printing of colonial scrip.

Term #5: Stamp Act (1765)

The Stamp Act was another attempt by the British government to make colonists help pay for the French and Indian War. Passed by Parliament in 1765, it was a highly unpopular tax on printed matter ranging from legal contracts to newspapers to playing cards. Colonists vehemently condemned the Act as illegal because they had not been consulted—not even through their colonial legislatures—before its passage. They not only refused to use the required stamps, they formed mobs that harassed and intimidated the crown's stamp agents. Nine colonies sent representatives to the Stamp Act Congress that October. This congress, considered a precursor of the First Continental Congress of 1774, adopted a Declaration of Rights and Grievances and wrote petitions to King George III and Parliament. In the face of boycotts and a loss of trade revenue, Parliament repealed the Stamp Act in 1766.

Term #6: Sons of Liberty

The Sons of Liberty were various patriot groups that sprung up in all thirteen colonies in the summer of 1765 to resist the Stamp Act and similar British measures through petitions, pamphleteering, public meetings, organized protests, and staged vandalism. Although not a formal organization, the Sons of Liberty played an important role in turning public opinion against British taxation and repression in the decade before the Declaration of Independence, especially in Massachusetts and Virginia. Their rebellious activism led to outright war. The disguised protesters who carried out the Boston Tea Party in 1773 were the Sons of Liberty.

Term #7: The Intolerable Acts

Also called the Coercive Acts (primarily by the British), the Intolerable Acts were a series of four laws passed by Parliament in 1774 as an attempt to crack down on the colonists and punish them in response to the Boston Tea Party and the growing rebellion in Massachusetts. The laws were 1) the Boston Port Act, which shut down the Port of Boston; 2) the Massachusetts Government Act, which did away with elective government in Massachusetts, giving all positions to royal appointees; 3) the Administration of Justice Act, which authorized the transfer of any trial to London, meaning that British officers arrested for crimes against colonists could not be tried by Massachusetts courts; and 4) the Quartering Act, which required colonists to house British troops in their dwellings. The acts stirred outrage throughout the colonies, leading to the formation of the First Continental Congress.

Term #8: Taxation without representation

Colonies accused Parliament of illegally passing tax levies against people who were not eligible to vote in Parliamentary elections and thus had no say in the matter. The charge of taxation without representation resonated powerfully through the colonies and was another motive for revolution. Under the Enlightenment concept that government requires the consent of the governed, colonists saw the passage of new British taxes on them as unjustified. They believed that the only governmental bodies that could legally tax them were the bodies they elected: the various colonial legislatures. Colonists rejected the specious British argument that they enjoyed virtual representation in Parliament.

Term #9: Treaty of Paris (1783)

The Treaty of Paris, between the United States of America and Great Britain, formally ended the American Revolutionary War. Under the treaty, Great Britain officially recognized the thirteen colonies as free and sovereign states. The 1783 treaty should not be confused with many other treaties by that name, both earlier and later. The 1763 pact that ended the Seven Years War (and the French and Indian War) also was called the Treaty of Paris.

Term #10: Articles of Confederation (1781–1789)

The Articles of Confederation bound the thirteen original states into a loose confederation and functioned as the first U.S. constitution. They specified the powers of Congress but established no administrative structure for a strong federal government. Congress could regulate foreign affairs, conduct wars, deal with Native American tribes, run the postal service, and settle territorial disputes between states. Congress could request troops and money from the states but had no way to enforce its requests. In other words, the federal government was essentially powerless. By 1786, it was clear that the United States needed a much better constitution if it was to survive as a nation. The Constitutional Convention, called to rectify the matter, convened in Philadelphia in 1787.

Chapter Twelve

Mindy watched in horror as the chubby gray pigeon on the top branch of a nearby oak expanded like a helium balloon. Its fluffy feathers became stiff gray bristles . . . its beak an oversized snout with six-inch tusks . . . and its slender feet into the cloven hooves of a three-hundred-pound gray wild boar that released a terrified squeal as it plummeted the fifteen feet to the ground.

Its squeal terminated abruptly as it hit the brick sidewalk.

"How did a boar that size get into a tree?" Jonathan said, shaking his head.

"It was a pigeon," Mindy said.

He arched an eyebrow. "Are you certain, Mindy? It's a boar now—a dead boar, but still a boar."

The Minister's back had been to the oak tree, and he'd missed the entire transformation.

But Mindy hadn't. "It's Zuriel. It's got to be." She scanned the area for the stout Time Stream Investigation unit supervisor. "Where's Dewitt?"

"Let us not stay to find out," Jonathan said.

The boar's legs twitched in unison, and it let out a high, twisted squeal of pain.

"But he's hurt!" Mindy said.

"Which means he can't follow us when we depart."

"I'm not going to abandon an injured animal," Mindy said. "I volunteer at a vet clinic. I can help."

"And how many wild boars do you get at this . . . *vet* . . . clinic?"

"That's not the point. I can help. I know I can." Squealing and groaning, Zuriel struggled to regain his footing but could only rock on his side. A chorus of grunts and snorts bounced off the brick buildings that lined the thoroughfare.

"That doesn't sound good," Mindy said. She pulled the chronolyzer from the pocket beneath her skirt. "Chronolyzer, why are there other pigs in the middle of Philadelphia?"

THERE IS A 3.4 PERCENT PROBABILITY THAT THEY'RE NOT COMING TO EAT THEIR WOUNDED ADVERSARY.

"But Zuriel isn't even a real boar."

THEY DON'T KNOW THAT, ALTHOUGH THEY WON'T BE HAPPY TO GET A JAW FULL OF METAL AFTER THE FIRST COUPLE OF BITES.

"But why are they even here? This is a huge city."

YOU'VE OBVIOUSLY SEEN—AND SMELLED—THE GARBAGE-FILLED DITCHES THAT LINE MOST STREETS? IN COLONIAL AMERICA, PIGS ARE NOTCHED ON THE EAR TO INDICATE THE OWNER AND THEN ALLOWED TO FEED FREELY.

The urgent grunts and snorts sounded even closer now.

"Well, they're not going feed on Zuriel." Mindy approached the three-hundred-pound gray boar, his sides heaving with the effort of ragged breaths. She knelt and tentatively touched his coarse gray hair.

Zuriel writhed and squealed in pain but made no aggressive move toward Mindy.

"Jonathan, we need to get Zuriel somewhere safe."

"We need to get *ourselves* somewhere safe. Dewitt could arrive any second."

"Help me move him."

"He weighs more than both of us combined!"

Mindy peered into Zuriel's tortured gray eyes. "You have to morph into something smaller, so we can carry you. Transform into a cat or something."

Zuriel's snout retracted and grew whiskers, then immediately popped back out.

"Chronolyzer, why isn't he transforming?"

THE DAMAGE FROM THE FALL IS TOO EXTENSIVE. IT APPEARS HE HAS ENOUGH ENERGY TO TRANSFORM BUT NOT TO PERFORM THE CALCULATIONS REQUIRED TO MAINTAIN THE NEW STATE. HE SHOULD REGAIN THIS ABILITY ON HIS OWN AS HE HEALS.

"Can you do the calculations for him?"

DONE, the chronolyzer typed.

The boar was gone, and in his place, a short-haired gray cat lay on his side, gasping. Mindy gently cradled him in her arms. She turned to Jonathan. "Now we can go."

This time Mindy rode behind Jonathan on the white mare so that she could keep an eye on Zuriel the cat.

ZURIEL SAYS THANK YOU FOR RESCUING HIM, the chronolyzer typed, AND THAT WE NEED TO HEAD TWENTY-SIX DEGREES NORTHWEST IN ORDER TO REACH WIDOW MADISON'S BOARDINGHOUSE. IN HUMAN-SPEAK, THAT MEANS TURN LEFT AT THE NEXT CORNER.

"You can talk to him?"

HE WAS DESIGNED WITH A CHRONOLYZER INTERFACE. ALTHOUGH CYBER-BLOODHOUNDS CAN NORMALLY TRANSFORM AT WILL, THEY CAN ALSO HAVE TRANSFORMATION FORCED ON THEM LIKE WE DID TO HIM JUST NOW.

Jonathan guided the horse slowly along the path Zuriel provided to avoid jostling the injured animal. "Will the cat recover?" he asked.

"I think so. There's no blood, and his breathing isn't raspy, so he probably doesn't have a punctured lung. He might have a few broken ribs, but I could wrap them with one of my petticoats to help them heal."

"Perhaps we should do that—and leave him someplace safe."

"He won't be able to defend himself if he gets in trouble."

"Mindy, you are forgetting that we have, in essence, just stolen our pursuer's best weapon against us. If Zuriel can talk to our chronolyzer, what is to stop him from relaying our location to Dewitt's chronolyzer?"

"But we just saved him."

The chronolyzer broke in. ZURIEL SAYS DEWITT MADE HIM FALL OUT OF THE TREE.

"Dewitt pushed him out of the tree?"

ZURIEL HAD BEEN INSTRUCTED TO TAKE THE FORM OF A PIGEON AND MONITOR OUR POSITION UNTIL DEWITT COULD RENDEZVOUS WITH HIM. WHEN THE TSI SUPERVISOR FOUND OUT WE WERE ABOUT TO MOVE AGAIN, DEWITT INSTRUCTED ZURIEL TO DETAIN US AND FORCED HIS TRANSFORMATION INTO THE BOAR WHILE ZURIEL WAS STILL IN THE TREE.

"How could he be so cruel?" Mindy said.

ZURIEL SAYS EVEN IF WE CHOOSE TO LEAVE HIM, HE WILL NOT RETURN TO DEWITT.

"We're not leaving you," Mindy said, stroking Zuriel's head.

He purred.

Lulled by the sleeping cat's warmth and the swaying gait of the horse, Mindy allowed herself to relax as Jonathan took them back toward the boardinghouse.

They dismounted down the street from Widow Madison's place, stopping to return the dainty white mare. The two-person chaise carriage remained, but instead of hitching her back up, they tied her lead to a nearby tree.

She pranced uneasily.

"Shhh . . . it's okay. No heavy carriages for you tonight," Mindy murmured, patting the horse. "You've worked hard enough."

Widow Madison's boardinghouse loomed silent and foreboding down the street. A single candle burned in an upstairs window.

The white mare snorted, pulling back on her lead.

"So how should we proceed?" Jonathan said, joining Mindy as she stroked the unconscious Zuriel.

"One thing's for sure—after the lies Dewitt told about us, they're not going to be happy to see us at the boardinghouse," Mindy said.

A coarse, brazen voice came from behind them. "I wouldn't wager on that."

Something hard whacked Mindy across the back of her head.

The world went black.

Justify My Loss:

3 of Britain's Excuses for Losing the Revolutionary War

They had the best-trained troops and the best weapons—not to mention the spiffiest uniforms. So how did the greatest military force in the world lose to a bunch of poorly trained (and poorly dressed) patriots?

Excuse #1: Blame France!

Simply put, French support made all the difference for the Americans. Fearing that a British victory would threaten French possessions in the Caribbean, France's King Louis XVI promised supplies, troops, and ships to the patriots. French troops and a French naval blockade at Yorktown, Pennsylvania, eventually helped force the surrender of British general Charles Cornwallis, which ended the war. Once the French signed on, other nations followed, including Spain, which declared war in 1779. Add the Dutch to the list of allies and, well, things began to get a little dicey for the Brits.

Excuse #2: Blame Ireland!

You think the colonists had issues with England? Ireland's resentment ran much deeper. English rule had begun in the late twelfth century, and the mistreatment was far harsher than anything the Americans had experienced. In the eighteenth century, England imposed a "Protestant ascendancy" in an overwhelmingly Catholic Ireland, which meant that only Protestants could be elected to the Irish Parliament or serve in other government posts. And even Irish Protestants rankled under new rules that allowed the English Parliament to legislate Ireland and gave the English House of Lords a supreme court role in Irish legal matters. This legacy of shared oppression led the Irish Parliament in 1768 to pass symbolic resolutions sympathetic to the American colonists. The war in America forced England to remove government troops from Ireland—a somewhat risky move, since it left Ireland vulnerable to attack, especially by the French, in a time when Britain was at war on several fronts. It became necessary for the English to authorize the formation of local militias so that the island would not be defenseless. Many in Parliament feared the absence of English military strength would compromise England's control of Ireland. They knew that anti-English feelings ran deep and that Irish militia units, as useful as they might prove against French incursions, could also turn to insurrection or even outright revolution.

Excuse #3: Blame the British Prime Minister!

When Lord Frederick North became prime minister of Great Britain in 1770, the majority of American colonists weren't necessarily calling for independence. North helped change all that. He ignored the outcry over the controversial tax policy that eventually led to the Boston Tea Party and responded to the protests by passing the Intolerable Acts, which restricted American trade and generally whipped up support for revolution. North failed to recognize the extent of discontent among the colonies, sorely underestimated American resolve, and failed to come up with a plan to avoid war until it was too late. Although North tried repeatedly to resign from 1777 on, the king pleaded with him to stick it out. But after the surrender of British general Cornwallis in 1781, he'd had enough. The prime minister was forced to make his exit and, in the end, Parliament blamed North—perhaps as much as they blamed the king—for the loss of the American colonies.

Chapter Thirteen

Mindy awoke with a headache. Greasy ropes bound her wrists and ankles. Everything smelled of mulch. She squinted, and her claustrophobic quarters fuzzed into focus.

Jonathan, similarly bound and awake, lay next to Mindy on a dirt floor. A wall of split firewood towered on the other side of him. No sign of Zuriel, although Mrs. Double-Tripe's transplanted nest rested in one corner. They were in Widow Madison's woodshed. Two large upended logs served as stools for Mindy and Jonathan's captors, who swapped flasks with gusto.

Peyton Lynch clapped his confederate on the shoulder. "Hey, Samuel, they're awake."

"Gluckish," Samuel said. "Now that we know they're not dead we can go collect the reward."

Peyton crouched down, wobbling only inches from Mindy's face. "Eight pounds each," he said, his breath reeking of his appropriated wine. "Your master's offering eight pounds *specie* each for you. You must be a prime piece for him to offer so much."

"Please don't turn us over to Dewitt," Mindy begged.

"Okay," Peyton said. "If you give us *sixteen* pounds . . . *each*."

Both young men guffawed. Evidently sixteen pounds was a rather large amount.

After hearing Peyton tell of his contraband smuggling efforts with their loyalist neighbor, Mindy could believe the slacker might ruin people's lives for a few quick bucks. But Samuel had shown himself to be a kind, even-tempered, good man in the short time Mindy had known him. Poverty could make you desperate, but it didn't change who you were inside.

"No money?" Samuel asked, taking a worn rag from his pocket. "Boo-hoo." He gagged Mindy with the foul-tasting scrap and did the same to Jonathan.

"We'll be back in the morning, after we receive our just payment from your master," Peyton said, slurring almost every word.

Samuel crouched down, tugging at Mindy's ropes. "All snug for the night—but what's this?" Samuel reached into the folds of Mindy's skirt and pulled out the chronolyzer. "I can't leave you with this. Sleeping on a chronolyzer all night would have put a mean crick in your back."

Mindy's eyes widened. Andros. Only the chronopolice and the body-hopping fairy knew about chronolyzers, and last time she checked, Samuel wasn't a Time Stream Investigator.

"And without it," Samuel continued, "I can't extract Glitta—my Galagian employer—when I find out which boarder she's in."

Peyton held his flask above his head with both hands and peered at the cap. "It's empty!" he said, shaking it.

"Try taking the cork out, lempke," Samuel said, as the two men shut the door to the woodshed, leaving Mindy and Jonathan in darkness. The only sound was the rustling of Mrs. Double-Tripe and her twelve baby mice.

Mindy struggled against her ropes and heard Jonathan doing the same. Nothing budged. In the night where no one could see her cry, Mindy released the tears of rage and frustration she'd been fighting back almost since they'd arrived in Philadelphia.

Jasper was right. Dewitt said Jasper blamed her for making bad choices that affected the team. It was all her fault. She knew that now. All the good intentions in the world didn't mean squat when your little sister was about to die. It was all Mindy's fault.

Mindy cried until she'd run out of tears, finally falling asleep a few hours before dawn.

* * *

An earsplitting yowl woke Mindy. Daylight licked the woodshed.

A second keening shriek made Mindy wish her hands were untied just so she could cover her ears. Insistent claws scratched at the door, and then a single gray paw reached beneath and tried to pull it open. Zuriel had found them!

On the other side of the door, Bridget shouted, "Shoo!"

"We'll save you and your babies, Mrs. Double-Tripe!" Sarah cried.

Two paws dug furiously beneath the door.

"Stop that!" Sarah said.

Despite the ribs he'd broken the previous night, Zuriel squeezed underneath the door and darted to Mindy. Bridget flung the door open, broom in hand, with a panting Sarah right behind her.

"Mindy! Jonathan! What happened to you?" Sarah cried as she and Bridget sprang to untie them.

Mindy spat the filthy rag out of her mouth. "We came back for something we'd forgotten, and Peyton and Samuel knocked us out and tied us up in here."

Bridget laughed. "Why in blazes would they do that?"

"For the reward money," Jonathan said, rubbing his abraded wrists. "They left us here so they could go find Dewitt and claim it."

"You'd better leave before they come back, then," Bridget said.

"No," Mindy said. "I need to get the thing I came for. It's in the house."

"Widow Madison isn't going to like this," Sarah said.

Before they left the shed, Mindy scooped up Mrs. Double-Tripe's nest. Because of Zuriel's digging, the woodshed was no longer a safe place for baby mice.

As they crossed the backyard, Mindy heard a commotion out on the street. Soldiers on horseback rode alongside carriage after carriage of wealthy, well-groomed men.

It sounded like the procession Dr. Franklin had asked her to attend—not that she'd do anything of the sort after rolling around in the dirt on the woodshed floor all night. She wondered if he'd notice her absence.

"What's going on out there?" Mindy asked.

"The Light Horse of the City of Philadelphia, the new cavalry, is escorting the delegates to Second Continental Congress to the State Building. Their first session is today," Sarah said.

"In other words," Bridget said, "a bunch of stiff-rumped, purse-prouds are flaunting their blue blood before they go into hiding so they can tell the rest of us what to do."

Sarah sighed. "You've been spending too much time with Mr. Winsley."

Inside, Widow Madison slid a pot of something onto a hook on the side of the giant kitchen fireplace as Mr. Winsley kept her company picking oakum in the corner. "Time is not to be wasted, girls," Widow Madison said, poking into her pot with a wooden spoon. "The fire is dying because of your delay with the kindling."

Mindy decided the only thing she could do was to throw herself on Widow Madison's mercy and hope she'd let them stay around long enough that she could find Serena. Zuriel the cat rubbed up against her legs in support.

With as much humility and sincerity as she could muster, Mindy said, "I'm sorry to trouble you, Widow Madison, but—"

The plump Quaker frowned and turned toward her, but when she saw Mrs. Double-Tripe's nest of newborns cupped in Mindy's hands, Widow Madison screamed and dropped the wooden spoon into the pot.

"It's just Mrs. Double-Tripe and her babies," Mindy said, extending the nest toward her.

"Get them away from me!" she shouted, backing away.

"But I thought you liked mice."

A confused look glazed Widow Madison's round face. "I do, I mean I did, I mean—" Quivering, she peered into the nest just as Mrs. Double-Tripe reared up to display her displeasure at having her babies jostled.

Widow Madison ran into the front parlor shouting, "Get that stupid aqua-rat out of here!"

The hairs on the back of Mindy's neck stood up. *Get that stupid aqua-rat out of here.* That was what Serena had said when she found Mindy's hamster Chewie swim in their bathtub.

"Jonathan, we've found her!" Mindy cried. "Serena's inside Widow Madison!"

Timeline:

A Tale of Two Georges

Ancient Greece 1657 1732 1738 1740 1753 1754 1760 1762 1763 1764–65

The name George, meaning "farmer," makes its first appearance.

1657 1732 1738 1740 1753 1754 1760 1762 1763 1764–65 1769 1775 1776 1781 1787

John Washington, great-grandfather of George Washington, sails from his native England to seek his fortune in the new colony of Virginia.

1657 1732 1738 1740 1753 1754 1760 1762 1763 1764–65 1769 1775 1776 1781 1787

A son is born to planter Augustine Washington and his second wife, Mary, in Westmoreland County, Virginia. Patriotic British subjects, they name the baby George, after England's King George II.

1657 1732 1738 1740 1753 1754 1760 1762 1763 1764–65 1769 1775 1776 1781 1787

A son is born to Frederick Louis, Prince of Wales, and Princess Augusta of Saxe-Gotha in London. They name the baby George William Frederick.

1657 1732 1738 1740-ish 1753 1754 1760 1762 1763 1764–65 1769 1775 1776 1781

A young George Washington *does not* chop down his father's cherry tree and confess to the deed. Got it? It never happened. Sheesh.

Young Virginia militia leader George Washington leads a party into the western wilderness to warn French soldiers not to encroach on the Ohio River Valley. The French tell him to buzz off.

Throughout May and July, George Washington, now a colonel in command of 160 Virginia militiamen, leads a surprise attack on a French-occupied fort at what will later be Pittsburgh, sparking the French and Indian War. The French retaliate and, after an all-day fight, Washington is forced to surrender.

Upon the death of his grandfather, George William Frederick becomes king of England, officially changing his name to George III, or GIII to friends.

George III begins to suffer from bouts of illness that will continue for the rest of his life. His symptoms include insomnia, a rapid pulse, and fever. His doctors are baffled, having apparently failed to notice the gigantic stash of Red Bull by the king's bed.

George III's prime minister, conveniently also named George, argues that the American colonies should pay more in taxes to support the cost of their defense by British forces.

Prime Minister George Grenville gets more taxes passed, including the Sugar Act and the Stamp Act.

George Washington, in a letter to fellow Virginia legislator (and fellow George) George Mason, expresses his willingness to take up arms, if necessary, against the British. The correspondence went something like: "George, we've just gotta stop George and George." "Absolutely, George; these other Georges are mucking everything up." "Great, George, glad to have you on board. George."

On April 19, the Second Continental Congress appoints George Washington commander-in-chief of colonial military forces.

The Second Continental Congress votes to approve the Declaration of Independence on July 4. Forgetting to check his RSS newsfeed that day, George III writes in his diary, "Nothing important happened today." He finds out about the whole independent colonies thing a couple of weeks later when the news arrives by ship.

On Christmas Day, George Washington ferries a force of 2,400 men across the Delaware River from Pennsylvania into New Jersey where, at the Battle of Trenton, he surprises and defeats a garrison of Hessian soldiers fighting for the British.

On October 19, George Washington forces British general Charles Cornwallis to surrender at the end of the three-week siege of Yorktown, Virginia. The Revolutionary War ends.

On May 13, George Washington is unanimously elected president of the Constitutional Convention in Philadelphia, the group charged with creating the constitution for the new nation.

George III suffers an attack of liver trouble, accompanied by temporary mental derangement. Normally a pretty polite guy, he begins shouting obscenities and cursing the queen.

On April 16, George Washington is unanimously elected president of the United States by a group of electors. Two weeks later, he is inaugurated on Wall Street in the nation's new capital, New York City.

George Washington dies on December 14, two years after finishing his second term as president.

George III suffers through several bouts of illness that grow more frequent and more severe. Between episodes, he continues to be perfectly lucid and healthy. Eventually, however, he appears to go permanently mad.

George III dies. His son, yet another George, becomes King George IV. Lil'

George, who has been acting as king since 1811, takes the news in stride, although he is reportedly thrilled about finally getting to wear that snazzy crown.

It's a new century, and the Georges continue their stunning reign of domination when *George of the Jungle,* the Saturday morning animated cartoon series, debuts on ABC television. Despite lasting only seventeen episodes, it becomes a cult classic that inspires a big-screen movie adaptation thirty years later, followed by a sequel in 2003, neither of which is very good.

Boy George, cross-dressing lead singer of the English pop group Culture Club, is catapulted to celebrity when the band's single "Do You Really Want to Hurt Me?" hits #1 on charts around the world.

The new political magazine *George,* brainchild of presidential son John F. Kennedy, Jr., debuts. Excited to finally have a magazine about them, Georges across the country are disappointed to discover that *George* is really just a stylish, celebrity-focused political magazine.

The new millennium promises no end to the rule of the Georges as George W. Bush ascends to the throne of America.

Chapter Fourteen

Mindy thrust the mouse nest into Mr. Winsley's lap. "Hold these for me," she said, dashing after Widow Madison. Everyone but Mr. Winsley followed.

"Serena?" Mindy asked softly. "Is that you?"

Widow Madison collapsed on the sofa in front of the window, burying her hands in her face. "I'm so confused. There are so many different voices in my head." She looked up at Mindy, both tormented and terrified. "Do you think I'm possessed?"

Jonathan knelt at her side and took her hand. "You are not possessed, gentle woman, just befuddled."

She sniffed. "Why would I act like that? I love Mrs. Double-Tripe."

"Calm yourself," Jonathan said, patting her hand. "It will pass."

Mindy felt relieved that they'd found Serena before Andros had, but without the chronolyzer Samuel took from her, she couldn't send Serena back to the twenty-first century. She'd have to steal it back without alerting Samuel, whom Andros had possessed, that they'd found the host body.

Footsteps thundered down the front stairs. Peyton and Samuel charged into the room.

"What's wrong?" Samuel said.

Peyton groaned, obviously hung over. "Whoever screamed, do *not* do it again."

A brick crashed through the front window, whizzing inches from Sarah's rounded stomach. She staggered half a step backward and fell. Gasping, her eyes widened.

Samuel ran over to her, his brow knitting in worry. "Are you okay?"

"The—brick—the—"

"It's okay," he said. "It missed you . . . and your baby."

The seventeen-year-old grabbed at her stomach, breathing heavily. "No, no it's not okay," she said. "My baby is coming—right now."

From outside, Conrad Flaugh's cultured, authoritative voice of persecution boomed: "On behalf of their master, Mr. Dewitt, we demand you immediately relinquish the indentured servants and known Tories Mindy Gold and Jonathan Hartthorne."

Peyton cursed. "Now we'll never get our reward, Samuel."

The young laborer didn't leave Sarah's side. "What reward?"

"The one we heard last night was in the *Pennsylvania Gazette?*"

Samuel shook his head.

"The one that promised six pounds each for these runaway indentured servants?"

"Again, no."

Peyton sighed. "You should never get so boosey that you lose track of your money."

"It was eight pounds each," Mindy corrected, "and we're not Tories."

Outside, Dewitt stepped forward, away from the crowd.

Zuriel arched his back and hissed from the window.

"My indentured servants are filthy Tories who fled from my home in Virginia to fight with General Gage's British troops in Boston," Dewitt said.

Shocked silence enveloped the room. It was one thing to have a little tea now and then but another to fight in the King's Army.

The crowd booed and hissed. "Remember Concord!" someone shouted.

"Dewitt is lying," Jonathan said.

"And he has been the whole time," Mindy added.

"That's it!" Jonathan said, brightening. "He *has* been lying the whole time—but he just added one lie too many."

He turned to the boardinghouse owner, who hadn't moved from the sofa, lost in the voices inside her head. "Widow Madison, when Dewitt came to claim us the first time, what did he say about us?"

The glassy-eyed Quaker looked up. "That you and Mindy were in love and ran away to get married because he wouldn't let you."

Jonathan blushed. "But did he say anything about us being Tories?"

She shook her head. "No."

He turned toward the hung-over Peyton. "And in that notice you heard about, did *it* say we were Tories?"

Mindy held her breath. Jonathan was pushing it. Dewitt *could* have listed them as Tories in the advertisement.

"No, it didn't say you were Tories."

Jonathan smiled. "But he says it now. Why is that?"

Mindy said, "Because the parade for the Second Continental Congress delegates got everyone all wound up. Dewitt was smart enough to know he could only get that patriotically charged mob to threaten us is if he labeled us enemies of America."

Outside, the crowd's unrest escalated. "Do not let your inaction place you on the wrong side, Widow Madison," Conrad shouted.

Sarah cried out as another contraction hit her.

"Let's get her off the floor," Mindy said to Samuel. As they helped the teen to the sofa, Mindy eyed his suit for funny lumps or square corners that might reveal the chronolyzer.

Nothing.

Outside on the street, someone in the mob brandished a small barrel of tar; another carried a bag of feathers.

"I'm leaving," Jonathan said.

Mindy's stomach twisted. "What?"

"Violence seems inevitable and imminent. I hope to draw the mob away from here long enough to give Sarah time to have her child and you time to retrieve that which you lost."

"You don't know enough about Philadelphia to outrun locals."

"She's right," Samuel said. "A mob will catch one man, but if it has to split its efforts between two, it will be more difficult. I will go with you."

"And what if the mob had *three* people to hunt?" Bridget offered, her tomboy swagger resurfacing. "Let them chase me. I've done nothing wrong."

Peyton sighed. "Well, I *have* done something wrong—quite a few things, actually—so I'll run too, but I don't plan on coming back, or on getting snapt."

Widow Madison's ashen skin glistened with sweat. "I don't think I can run anywhere right now," she said.

"You'll stay here with me to help Sarah with the baby," Mindy said, although what she really meant was that Widow Madison could stay here while she found the chronolyzer and sent Serena back to the twenty-first century.

Widow Madison nodded vaguely.

Samuel, Peyton, Bridget, and Jonathan gathered around the back door, planning their routes. Mr. Winsley, unable to follow all the commotion by hearing alone, had fallen asleep on his stool, the mice still on his lap.

"Jonathan, don't go," Mindy blurted. "I know we're out of options, and I know you're not afraid, but I just don't want you to go." A lump formed in her throat.

"I'll come back to you," he said.

"Not if they catch you, you won't."

"If they catch me, you will come for me." It was a statement, not a question. "You are the most competent woman I have ever met, Mindy Gold. We have bound our fates together many times in our travels, and I could not live another day if you lost Serena because I didn't do everything in my power to help."

"But—"

"Go save your sister," Jonathan said, his emerald green eyes burning with an intensity she'd never seen before. In a single swift motion he pulled her against his chest and kissed her.

"I'll come back," he whispered. "I promise."

He released her, and before Mindy could protest further, Jonathan strode out the back door.

Bordering on Silly:

6 Fun Facts About the 13 Colonies

In an alternate U.S. universe, Maryland could be Henriettaland, Vermont could be its own nation, and Connecticut residents could root for the Buckeyes.

Fun fact #1: Nearly half the colonies took their names from English royalty

In colonial times, it was customary to name new settlements after English monarchs or their royal relatives. But the name game wasn't always so straightforward. When colonists decided to honor Queen Elizabeth I by naming a colony after her, they adapted her famous nickname, "the Virgin Queen," into *Virginia*. The Carolinas were named for Charles II, New York was named for King James II (who was also the Duke of York), and Georgia is an adaptation of George II's name. The most surprising name of all? Maryland, which is *not* named for a Queen Mary. The state is actually named for Queen Henrietta Maria, wife of King Charles I. Guess the colonists thought Maryland had more of a ring to it than Henriettaland.

Fun fact #2: There is no state named Rhode Island

Okay, it's a technicality, but Rhode Island's name isn't "Rhode Island." It's "Rhode Island and Providence Plantations." Clocking in at five words, that's the longest name of any state. Incidentally, Rhode Island is not an island, although the state does include several islands. Among the original thirteen states, three call themselves "commonwealths" instead of "states"—the Commonwealth of Pennsylvania, the Commonwealth of Massachusetts, and the Commonwealth of Virginia.

Fun fact #3: The Carolinas used to be super-sized

Imagine a state with a northern border of North Carolina, a southern border of Georgia, and a western border of . . . the Pacific Ocean? In 1665, King Charles I gave those boundaries to the Colony of Carolina. Although it sounds ridiculous, it was not uncommon in those days for royal land grants to lay claim to vast expanses of land. That way, a country or a colony would be in a better position to jockey for more territory in future land disputes. The Carolina border never quite made it to the Pacific. In fact, even the small slice of eastern territory proved too big to administer and, in 1729, it was divided into the present North and South Carolinas.

Fun fact #4: Vermont used to be an independent nation

In 1777, Vermont declared itself a self-governing republic called the Republic of Vermont, and it remained that way until 1791, when it joined the Union as the fourteenth state. Vermont never won diplomatic recognition from any actual country, so its claim to nationhood was a bit shaky—as was that of the short-lived Republic of West Florida, a stretch of land encompassing parts of present-day Louisiana, southern Mississippi, and southern Alabama. In 1810, English-speaking residents there rebelled against Spain, which claimed the area as part of Spanish Florida. After overpowering a garrison of twenty-eight sleeping Spanish soldiers, the rebels declared a republic, only to be annexed by the U.S. government thirty-four days later. California also briefly declared itself a republic at the start of the Mexican-American War in 1846. However, only Texas and Hawaii can claim to have been formally recognized as independent republics before becoming states. The Republic of Texas lasted from 1836 to 1845 and the Republic of Hawaii from 1894 to 1898.

Fun fact #5: Maine used to be part of Massachusetts

Last time we checked, a certain piece of land—namely, New Hampshire—separated Maine from Massachusetts. It seems improbable, but from 1652 all the way up to 1820, Maine was officially part of Massachusetts, even though the two territories don't touch. There was always a strong urge in what was then the District of Maine, especially among the rugged settlers of the interior, to break away from Massachusetts. The district's independence movement stalled until the War of 1812, when British detachments from Canada conducted raids on Maine virtually unopposed. Angry that Massachusetts militia had not protected them, Maine residents demanded separation. Although it had been within the United States of America from the beginning, the district was finally admitted in 1820 as the twenty-third state, after Alabama in 1819 and before Missouri in 1821. So although Maine was *part* of one of the original thirteen states, it wasn't *one* of them.

Fun fact #6: Small states, like Connecticut, used to claim large territories out West

Massachusetts's western territories included east-to-west strips on either side of Lake Michigan—land that would later be included in the states of Michigan and Wisconsin. Connecticut claimed a narrower but longer strip extending through northern Pennsylvania and including bits of what would later be Ohio, Indiana, Michigan, and Illinois. Pennsylvania disputed Connecticut's claim, but it lasted—as did other such western claims— beyond the Revolutionary War. Through the 1780s and 1790s, most eastern states, unwilling to bear the costs of administering so much land, ceded their western claims to the new federal government. The huge, westernmost county of Virginia became the state of Kentucky. Western North Carolina became Tennessee. The Great Lakes region became the Northwest Territory until its growing population justified the formation of new states.

Chapter Fifteen

Almost instantly someone in the mob out front shouted, "They're trying to escape!"

Mindy's heart sank.

But the crowd broke apart chaotically as smaller groups pursued each person. The plan was working.

Now all Mindy had to do was find that stolen chronolyzer. She checked on Sarah and Widow Madison. Sarah's contractions had slowed, and she was resting on the couch with her eyes closed. Widow Madison sat stiffly in a chair next to her.

"I've got to go look for something upstairs," Mindy said. "Yell if you need me."

"Why would *I* need you?" Widow Madison said, her tone all Serena's. "You're not the boss of me."

Mindy suppressed a smile. Yeah, Serena was in there all right. "Sorry. I'll be right back." She headed for the stairs, and Zuriel followed along behind her. "Not very catlike, Zuriel," Mindy said as she climbed the stairs. The chronolyzer could very well be in Samuel's room, but if it wasn't, it wouldn't take long to search an empty house.

But, when she reached the second floor landing, she discovered she wasn't alone. Dewitt was in the hall pouring oil over the already sticky masses of oakum Mindy and the girls had left in their room.

"Ah, Miss Gold . . . what good fortune," he said, his smile as slick as the oil that oozed down the stairs.

"I'm not going back with you—not yet. My sister's inside Widow Madison. All I need is a chronolyzer to pull her out, so if you don't mind, I'll borrow yours." She reached out for the chronolyzer, but Dewitt snatched it away.

"I've no time for more of your shenanigans. Maybe your sister is inside of Widow Madison, and maybe she's not. I'm simply going to transport everyone back to 2512 and sort it out there. Once I extract the alien and the teen, I'll donate the colonial bodies to the Organ Factory."

Mindy shuddered. Somehow she didn't think the Organ Factory produced the ballpark keyboards that played happy songs about Cracker Jacks.

"We can transport out of here as soon as I've burned this hovel to the ground," Dewitt said.

"Why are you doing this?" Mindy asked.

"To repair the damage to the time stream. You see, infecting everyone with smallpox was your *second* mistake. Your first was helping extinguish the boardinghouse fire. If you hadn't spotted the blaze as quickly as you did, the chronolyzer estimates that everyone in the boarding-house would have either died in the fire or died fighting it. Though you infected some of the boarders with smallpox, none of them, it appears, will die from it, and that doesn't restore balance to the flow of the time stream. I'm here to make sure it appears as if everyone dies—"

"So you can give their bodies to the Organ Factory?" Mindy snapped.

Dewitt beamed. "Exactly! Now you're getting it."

The TSI supervisor's glib disregard for human life struck a chord.

"You're Andros, aren't you?"

Dewitt shook his head. "What? Andros? I'm going to all this trouble to bring your sister home without sending a tsunami onto the shores of history, and you accuse me of being possessed by that scum? How *dare* you." He punctuated his last sentence with a poke of the chronolyzer.

Zuriel the cat leapt straight up between the two of them and sunk his teeth into Dewitt's forearm. The TSI supervisor dropped the chronolyzer, and Mindy grabbed it.

The red panic button on the bottom of the chronolyzer screen tempted her. If there was ever a time to panic, it was now. Jasper had told her never to press it unless he was dead. Well, after what he had said to Dewitt about her, he was dead to her.

She pressed the button.

Jasper Gordon appeared in front of her, the sleeves of his white dress shirt rolled up and a stack of translucent file envelopes still in his arms.

Mindy folded her arms across her chest. "What are *you* doing here?"

For once in his life, Jasper wasn't restrained. He threw his arms around her. "Sure and I knew you wouldn't listen to me! You never do!"

She pushed him away.

Jasper frowned. "What's wrong?"

Behind Jasper, Dewitt started padding down the stairs.

"Zuriel, stop him!" Mindy said.

The cat leapt once more at Dewitt. In midair he transformed into the large Irish wolfhound. He landed on Dewitt's back, knocking the man down the stairs and pinning him to the floor.

"Get him off of me! Get him off of me!" Dewitt cried.

Zuriel growled.

"Maybe you shouldn't have transformed him into a hog while he was on a tiny branch fifteen feet above the ground."

Dewitt turned white. "He was in a tree? I didn't know . . . "

"Do you know what sound a three-hundred pound hog makes when he hits the ground from that high up?"

Dewitt looked genuinely upset.

Good, Mindy thought.

Stunned, Jasper said, "Mindy, get the dog off my boss."

"He's possessed by Andros. He acts just like him."

Dewitt tried to ease away from Zuriel, but the dog growled. "I'm not possessed. I'm not." His old bravado reappeared. "Jasper Gordon, if you don't get this dog off of me immediately, you'll never work again."

"Sure and I'm not working now, thanks to you." Jasper threw the file folders onto the floor. "Fecking files. We've got Andros on the loose, and you stick me in the plasticite basement filing forms out of sheer spite, you stupid gobshites." He turned to Mindy. "So what's going on?"

"What's going on with *you*? Is it true what Dewitt said—that you're *Andros's brother?*"

Jasper's eyes widened in surprise. He whistled. "So, the officious bastard told you, did he?"

"So it's true! You lied to me. And you're really not . . . human?"

"Sure and I'd have told you if I could, Mindy girl. I am indeed one of the fey. It's one of the things I'm not permitted to divulge about myself. If you hadn't noticed, those chronofascists do a pretty good job of restricting my range of actions and all."

"But I thought you told me Andros was an alien. Was that all a lie too?"

"Em. Now, I never said he was an alien, exactly. I said he was *working* with aliens. There's a difference."

"And are *you* working with them?"

"Shite no, girl. Andros is indeed my brother, but we've got feck all in common with each other. He's what you'd call a *pookah*—a mischievous sprite. He gets it from our mother. I'm a straight up pixie, just like my da'."

"That's . . . nice, I guess."

"Sure and the pixies are all forced to work for the great Free Fascist State of the future and all, but good luck trying to impress the pookahs into service. Ol' Andros offered his services to the Galagians as a way of overthrowing the State and plunging the world into chaos."

"Dewitt said you didn't really care about finding my sister."

"Sure and if I didn't care about Serena, would I have stolen this from HQ and hidden it on me person?"

"What is it?"

Jasper beamed. "Why, the smallpox antidote, of course."

Mindy grabbed the pixie and hugged him hard, knocking him off balance. "Oh, Jasper, I'm sorry I doubted you!" She used the chronolyzer to dial Jasper some period clothes and updated him in under a minute, while telling him her most important discovery—her sister. "So I'm certain Serena is inside of Widow Madison. All I have to do is get her to drink that last dose of tempose and transport her home."

Jasper nodded. "And after Serena's safe, we'll go find Jonathan."

Mindy smiled. "I'm glad you're here," she said quietly.

"You seem to have gotten along fine without me," he said, but his tone revealed his true appreciation.

They sealed Dewitt in a supervisor-sized plasticite body-baggy that Jasper summoned with the chronolyzer and left Zuriel to guard him before starting downstairs to retrieve Serena from Widow Madison and send her home. Halfway down, they heard the muffled sounds of a struggle and ran the rest of the way.

Widow Madison lay on the floor as Sarah, still pregnant, straddled her, pinning her hands with her knees.

"Sarah, what are you doing?" Mindy cried.

"What does it look like I'm doing, dear Mindy?" she said with a wicked smirk.

Only one person smirked quite like that. Only one. "Andros?" Mindy asked hesitantly.

"None other." The evil pookah forced the pregnant girl to smile and wink at Mindy.

Number Crunching:

13 Stats About the Revolution

Who says math is too hard? In this list, we really do a number on Revolutionary War history.

4 copycat "tea parties"

When those trend-setting Sons of Liberty dumped 90,000 pounds of English tea into Boston Harbor in December 1773, they inspired the spirit of rebellion in other disgruntled colonists—and even spawned copycats. Just months later, in March 1774, a less-publicized tea dump took place in Boston Harbor, followed by others in New York, Annapolis, and Greenwich, New Jersey.

5 civilians killed in the Boston Massacre

A handful of civilians died in the Boston Massacre on March 5, 1770, gunned down by British troops. After a British sentry struck a young Bostonian, a mob of dockworkers and others gathered, shouting epithets and throwing snowballs at the guard and other British soldiers. Eventually, the troops opened fire, hitting eleven men and killing five. Crispus Attucks, a merchant sailor and former slave, was the first to fall.

7 pounds of bread per week

Forget all that low-carb nonsense. A soldier in the Massachusetts militia received a weekly ration of seven pounds of bread, three and a half pints of peas, and four and two-thirds pounds of pork. When on the march, the weekly pork allowance increased to seven pounds and, instead of peas, soldiers received twenty-eight ounces of rum.

12 colonies voted to declare independence on July 2, 1776

Not every colony voted to ratify the Lee Resolution calling for independence. The lone holdout? New York, whose representatives bowed out because they wanted approval from their colonial assembly first. After getting the go-ahead, New York voted for independence on July 9.

35 years in the average lifespan

In seventeenth-century America, more than two out of every ten children died before reaching age ten. However, those who made it to their teen years had a reasonable chance of seeing age fifty, and some lived well into their eighties and nineties.

50 Massachusetts militiamen killed

Add five missing and thirty-nine wounded, and you have the casualty figures for the Massachusetts militia in the first military engagements of the Revolutionary War on April 19, 1775. British casualties numbered seventy-three dead, twenty-six missing, and 174 wounded.

56 signers of the Declaration of Independence

Of the fifty-six founding fathers who contributed their John Hancocks to the Declaration of Independence, two went on to become president: John Adams and Thomas Jefferson.

79 months of fighting

How long does it take to win a revolution? From the first shots fired at the battles of Lexington and Concord to the surrender of British general Charles Cornwallis on October 19, 1781, at the Siege of Yorktown, the fighting went on for six years and seven months.

About 2,400 troops crossed the Delaware River with George Washington

In December of 1775, Washington's regiment crossed the ice-strewn Delaware River for a sneak attack on the 1,400 Hessians and British troops camped in Trenton, New Jersey. This victory—in which 900 were taken prisoner—helped restore slumping American morale.

4,500 to 7,000 American soldiers killed in action

Estimates vary as to the total battle death toll of the Revolutionary War. Experts agree, however, that more died from disease and infection than from bullets or bombs. An estimated 25,000 Americans died of war-related causes. The Brits saw approximately 4,000 soldiers killed in combat, with a total casualty count of 70,000.

28,522 early Philadelphians

When the first U.S. census was conducted in 1790, Philadelphia was the second most populous city in the nation. The number-one most populous city in 1790? New York, with 33,131 residents. Today, New York remains the largest U.S. city with more than 8 million residents, while Philadelphia ranks fifth with about 1.5 million.

3,929,214 early Americans

My, how we've grown. In 1790, the U.S. population was inching toward 4 million. Almost two centuries later, the 2000 census reported that the number of Americans had reached 272,690,813, and today we have surpassed 300 million.

1,000,000,000 human beings on earth

The human population reached one billion around the year 1790. Only 184 years later, in 1974, there were three billion of us. And today's population of 6.5 billion is growing at a faster rate every day.

Chapter Sixteen

"Andros! It can't be you," Mindy cried. "We left you upstairs inside Supervisor Dewitt."

"Inside plasticite, I might add," Jasper said. "And in the history of time travel, no Galagian—or fairy—has ever body-hopped through plasticite."

Sarah shrugged. "Guess that wasn't me upstairs. If I were you, Jasper, I wouldn't expect a good raise at your next review."

"How did you find us?" Mindy asked.

Beneath Sarah, Widow Madison continued to struggle.

"You're terribly easy to track. Much easier than my alien friends, actually. I've discovered that it's simpler to just let you find the host body and then swoop on in and get my friend out. Of course I couldn't resist the smallpox." Andros made Sarah grin that awful crooked grin Mindy had seen on every other person he'd possessed.

"The smallpox?"

"Well, I needed a way to get into the house, didn't I? And possessing a mother and making her bring her smallpox-infected toddler to the house was much more interesting than just knocking on the door as a candle salesman or something equally lame."

"How could you let all those people get infected?"

"It's quite simple. The scabs are highly contagious, not to mention the pus from someone with active pustules." Andros grinned. "But I don't imagine that's what you're asking about, is it?"

"You're evil."

"*Au contraire*. The people *you* work for are evil. At least my brother has the excuse that they *force* him to work for them. What's yours? Now if you'll excuse me, I have to extract my Galagian friend, Glitta, from this fat slob of an innkeeper."

"But that will send my sister off to the Void."

Andros shrugged. "Can't be helped. You humans are always breeding. I imagine your parents will make another one."

"Serena, I know you're inside there somewhere," Mindy said. "I need your help. You have to fight the alien, keep control. Don't let it win. Don't!"

Widow Madison's arms dropped to her sides.

Andros grinned. "Looks like my girl Glitta's in control, not your bratty little sister."

Mindy knew what she had to do. It was risky, but she couldn't think of any other options. Galagians loved tempose, the chemical that enabled people to time-travel. Mindy already had more of it than a normal human. If she had even more . . .

Mindy took the vial of tempose she'd been carrying all this time and chugged it.

"You don't want that old woman," Mindy said. "You want me. My tempose levels are much higher."

Sarah sniffed the air like a bloodhound.

"And much tastier," Mindy added.

The pregnant girl collapsed.

Mindy's brain surged as if she'd drank five triple-lattés. The world felt different, brighter, more intense.

And more crowded.

When her fingers started wiggling on their own, she realized it wasn't the tempose. It was Andros.

Nice place you've got here, Andros said inside her head, *though a little bit too spacious for me. Empty heads are usually a bit too drafty to hang around in for too long.*

She had to fight him. She envisioned a clenched fist, and her fingers stopped wiggling and formed a fist.

Mindy watched the events unfold around her as if she were in a theater with the house lights on. Things happened, but not to her, and it was overall too industrially bright.

She tried not to let any of the physical changes distract her. Her only goal was to hold Andros.

The second Sarah collapsed, Jasper ran over to her and eased her onto her back on the floor. Widow Madison moaned as Jasper gave her the last required dose of tempose and began the calculations to send Serena home.

I hope we're not too late, Mindy thought.

Andros echoed in her head. *Why don't we walk on over and see for ourselves?*

Mindy's left foot lifted off the floor.

She forced it back down.

Stalemate.

You are definitely a dredger, Andros said.

The front door burst open, and Jonathan rushed into the parlor.

"Mindy, it's a miracle! Once the mob split up to pursue us, they stopped being a mob and started being people again. Most of them lost interest after a short time and went home. There are a few tenacious individuals, but I think all will be forgotten soon."

Mindy felt her head turn toward Minister Hartthorne. She gave him an odd, sideways grin and then winked at him.

The minister's always been good for a few laughs, Andros said inside her head. *Since you won't play nice, maybe I should give him another spin? He'll get my alien friend out of that Quaker.*

No! Mindy thought. *I won't let you do that to him again.* Andros had possessed Jonathan at the Battle of Bull Run and made him do horrible things that almost destroyed the Puritan minister.

As Mindy felt Andros pushing away from her, she pulled with everything she had. She imagined Andros being sucked down into the pit of quicksand in her mind. The more the pookah struggled, the deeper he sank.

"Almost there," Mindy heard Jasper say. "We've almost got Serena, and if you can hold Andros just a few more minutes, I can trap him as well. Just hold on."

Mindy couldn't believe it. After everything they'd gone through, she was finally going to be able to send her sister home, vanquish Andros, and maybe even go home herself. And maybe take Jonathan back with her.

Hope was her downfall. A split-second of distraction and human longing was enough to loosen her hold on Andros. In her quicksand mind, a green vine dropped in from above, hauling Andros up and out of her mind.

Mindy blacked out.

She woke up in Jonathan's strong arms. "She's safe, Mindy. Serena's home. Jasper finished the calculations right before you passed out."

"Should have let the chronolyzer do them," she said, smiling weakly. Her battle with Andros had taken everything out of her.

Jasper rolled his eyes. "Like it needs another thing to brag about."

"What about Andros? Did you catch him? Did I hold him long enough?"

Jonathan stroked her brow. "We'll get him next time."

Jasper turned pale. "If there's going to be a next time. We accused my boss of being an alien and sealed him in a big plastic baggy."

"Like he wasn't fresh enough already," Mindy joked.

Epilogue

When the team had returned to the safe room in 2512, Dewitt looked like an action figure that had been stuck in a bag of marshmallows and microwaved. They'd spent the last ten minutes trying to extricate him from the supervisor-sized body-baggy with mixed results.

"I'm going to be picking plasticite out of my hair for weeks," Dewitt said, his powdered colonial wig glued sideways on his head thanks to the liquefied goo.

"Sure and I'm awfully sorry, sir," Jasper said.

"We really thought you were possessed," Mindy said, plucking a chunk of plasticite from Dewitt's shoulder.

"Yes, yes, yes, so I've heard many times now," Supervisor Dewitt said.

The chronolyzer typed, THAT'S NUMBER TWENTY-SEVEN AND TWENTY-EIGHT IN THE LAST TEN MINUTES.

"Twenty-seven and twenty-eight what in ten minutes?" Jonathan asked confusedly.

INEFFECTUAL AND UNINSPIRED APOLOGIES.

Zuriel, now a silverback gray gorilla, picked plasticite from between Supervisor Dewitt's toes. The cyber-bloodhound and the tall, sticky fascist had made up when Zuriel found out that the flying hog thing was unintentional. Supervisor Dewitt just wasn't a dog person, cyborg or otherwise.

Back in 1776, with Serena and the alien Glitta out of her, Widow Madison was back to being a mouse person, though. She'd let Mrs. Double-Tripe and her family move back into the kitchen.

The entire boardinghouse was in a family mood thanks to Sarah's new baby boy. She named him Samuel, after her new fiancé.

True to his word, Peyton never returned to the boardinghouse, but Bridget did, mostly because she missed Mr. Winsley, whom she said reminded her of her grandfather.

While just down the street the Second Continental Congress made page after page of resolves concerning what would soon be a new nation, Widow Madison made one of her own. She resolved to listen more to her Inner Light and to help her growing boarding-house family listen to theirs so that they could all one day find peace and happiness.

Contentment, however, was not on Dewitt's agenda. He dug at his peeling, sticky arms. They'd suffered almost as much as his hair. Mindy spotted a large, fused strip on his forearm. She flicked up the edge with her fingernail, getting the strip started. "Ready, Supervisor Dewitt?" she asked.

"Ready for wha—"

Mindy ripped the entire strip in one quick motion.

Dewitt screamed.

"It's like a bandage. You have to go fast, or it hurts more."

The plasticite strip not only came up quickly, but it took with it all the hair on Dewitt's forearm.

Through gritted teeth Dewitt said, "I assure you, this could not possibly hurt more."

"Really?" Jasper said. "Sure and that's very interesting because the bandage hypothesis has been scientifically validated several times in independent experiments."

Jonathan nodded. "I can see the simplicity of it. Faster is better."

"Out!" Supervisor Dewitt raged. "I want all of you out of my sight! Now!"

Jasper hung his head. "Back to the Department of Eternal Misfiling?"

Mindy elbowed him in the ribs. The man didn't need any help picking a punishment for them, and there was still at least one teen who needed to be rescued from the effects of the chronobomb.

"That would mean you'd still be in my building," Supervisor Dewitt raged. "After all you've put me through, I don't want you within a hundred *years* of me, much less a hundred *yards*."

Using two fingers to hold the chronolyzer so that he wouldn't get plasticite on it, he said, "Chronolyzer, I want these yahoos back in the field immediately. Find them an assignment *at least* five hundred years in the past. Something far, far away—from me."

ASSIGNMENT SECURED, the chronolyzer typed. LIKELIHOOD OF NEW ASSIGNMENT BEING BETTER THAN PICKING PLASTICITE OFF YOUR BOSS: 99.99 PERCENT.

The chronolyzer screen went dark, and Mindy, Jasper, and Jonathan hurtled backward in time—toward their next assignment.

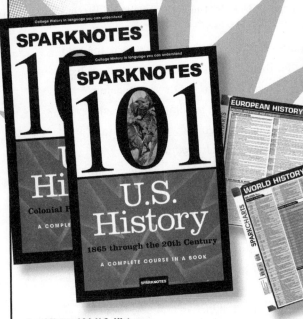